"Moss has mixed an expertly crafted cocktail of murder, mystery, and hedonism. *Mai Tais for the Lost* is a slick, sci fi-noir overflowing with memorable characters, gorgeous prose, and brilliant world building that will leave you thirsty for more."

— Joe Butler, author of *Of All Possibilities*

MAI TAIS
for the lost

A novella of
The Nightingale Electric Detective Agency

Mia V. Moss

Underland Press

This book is published by Underland Press, which is part of Firebird Creative, LLC (Clackamas, OR).

Send up a bottle of your best seaweed gin . . .

Edited by Mark Teppo
Book Design and Layout by Firebird Creative
Cover art elements by TiefenWerft & Viktoriia Protsak / stock.adobe.com

This Underland Press trade edition has an ISBN of 978-1-63023-065-4.

Underland Press
www.underlandpress.com

MAI TAIS
for the lost

For all the lost who found their way at Suki's

It was six in the evening and the sea above Electric Blue Moon was a riot of storm-tossed flotsam and unlucky fish. The call came in just as I was finishing the first round of a three-glass dinner of seaweed gin at Infinity's Cup, the favorite liquor cabinet of the habitat's young, reckless, and over-moneyed progeny.

Infinity Kovac himself was tending bar that night, slinging vintage trashy cocktails to classic house music in the moody purple light. He paused when my com buzzed next to my hand, the bottle of gin hovering a silent question over my empty glass. I glanced at the screen; it was Disco Bishop, my brother Rocket's fiancé. I nodded for Infinity to pour me another and picked up my com. I could polish off ten drinks before Disco was done talking.

"Marrow? Marrow, it's Disco."

His voice was strung higher than the lofty domed habitat roof. I sighed and motioned for Infinity to leave the bottle.

"Yeah, I know it's you Disco. What's the matter?"

"Rocket, he's—oh God, Marrow. I don't know how else to say it. Rocket's dead."

"Disco, baby, what do you mean Rocket's dead? I just saw him not two hours ago. He was fine. Perfectly healthy."

Rocket Nightingale was a force of nature. Young, beautiful, charismatic, wealthy as a king and generous as a saint.

His life was one unbroken stream of flashy parties and delightful adventures. He was also my older—and only— brother. He wasn't the kind of asshole to turn up dead out of the blue on an otherwise uneventful Wednesday.

"Someone *killed him*! I came home to change for a dinner party at the Van Houten's and there he was, sprawled out in the foyer with his skull in pieces and blood all over the tile and oh God, Marrow. The goddamned *foyer*!"

He cut off with a choked sob. I tried to find the bottom of my stomach, but it was as though some unseen hand had scooped it out every ounce of guts and left me scrambling for nothing but cold emptiness. When I finally found the air to speak, it was as though someone else had taken over my vocal cords. I sounded frosty smooth, alien in my own ears.

"Alright, honey. Stay right where you are, can you do that? I'm on my way now. Fix us both a strong drink while you wait." I sure as shit didn't need another, but it sounded like he could use one. It would keep him preoccupied for a little while, at least. "And Disco, don't call anyone else until I get there, alright?"

"S-sure, Marrow. No one else."

"*Especially* HabSec," I stressed. "No cops."

Disco knew better than to call HabSec, but a bad shock to the nerves can make people do stupid things. Habitat Security goons stomping all over a crime scene, attracting every tabloid in radio range, was the last thing we needed. I ended the transmission and stood up, pushing the bottle away. Infinity came over to settle up my tab and I held up a hand to stop him.

"Chances are high I'm just going to talk Disco down off the ceiling and be back inside an hour." I said. "And if not, I'll be seeing you tomorrow. Same time as always, pal."

Infinity nodded in time with the music, indifferent to the specifics of my emergency, and moved on to other patrons. I grabbed my things, pushed through the arriving after-work crowds, and caught a streetcar heading uptown.

Electric Blue Moon isn't the biggest and is definitely not the most technologically advanced habitat city in the Pacific, but it is the third oldest and comfortably ranks among the top five wealthiest. It was built and funded by the type of dynastic old money that likes to buy one hulking set of furniture for their mansion and pass it down through the generations, regardless of how out of fashion it is. Half of them are still using those same dead wood furnishings their ancestors lugged down with them to the bottom of the sea. The closets all came pre-lined with skeletons, too.

That old money is built into the DNA of the hab. The smell of dusty, hoarded cash perfumes the very atmosphere that circulates through the ventilation, breathed in and exhaled by a hundred thousand souls. It's a hardwood-and-gilded corners kind of place; a fantasia desperate to recall a surface-world myth that never existed in the first place. The electric streetcars even make old-timey clangy bell noises as they glide through foot traffic.

A serene synthetic voice announced my stop and I ran fingertips along the age-worn authentic wood paneling as I disembarked. The last cedars on the planet had probably been cut down to contribute such finishing touches.

When I got to Rocket and Disco's place, I nearly kept right on walking. HabSec's Chief Security Officer, Varsity Beckett, was waiting outside the gate in his ridiculous turquoise uniform and white sailor's scarf, looking real anxious to arrest someone for something. I could tell by the way he hefted his meatslab physique off the fence and rested one twitchy hand on his sidearm that he was hoping it'd be me.

My breath caught for the briefest of moments. If Hab-Sec was already on the scene . . . but no. My brother had been alive and healthy just hours ago. I could practically still smell his body wash from when he'd leaned in to tousle my hair as I left. I had been on the com with a client and my last gesture to my older brother had been to flip him off on my way out the door. I banished the thought with a scoff.

"If you're here to see Rocket, evidently you just missed him." I let my shoulder connect with his as I unlatched the gate and continued up the short walkway to the front door.

"Marrow Nightingale," Varsity spat, as though my name itself was a murder charge. "So quick with the quips. I've got some questions for you before you go inside."

"Give me a break, Varsity. I'm here about a family emergency."

"You just get here? Seems awfully convenient timing, you showing up right after the morgue picked up the body."

The body. Disco hadn't been hallucinating. My jaw clenched tight, but I refused to rise to Varsity's bait. I was well aware that anything I said would most certainly be used against me in his case write-up; he'd been looking for a way to get me off the hab ever since he'd picked up his badge.

It boils down to this. Electric Blue's got two types of bastards: rich ones and poor ones. There are the wealthy, and then there are the people who scrub the toilets of the wealthy. Or do their taxes. Sometimes both, if they're the kind of Poors with the right amount of hustle.

When everything went straight to Hell topside and the billionaires of Earth took refuge in the sea, they still needed their chefs, hair stylists, concierges, and housekeepers. And their HabSec Security Chiefs. Many of the toilet scrubbers have worked hard to build little work-er-bee dynasties of their own, working overtime to en-sure their children can live out of harm's way under the oceans.

But the threat of deportation to the surface always looms large. HabSec are police, judge, and execution-er, and there are two ways it's going to end for a body if they get caught breaking the rules: a hefty fine they'll never work off or a one-way ticket to the surface. In oth-er words, permanent exile. For you, your spouse, your kids—probably their kids, too, just to be thorough.

A twist of fate had elevated me, the humble daughter of service workers, out of reach from HabSec's threats and therefore out of their power. And if there was one thing men like Varsity hated more than anything, it was feeling impotent.

"I'm sure I don't know what you're insinuating, *Officer* Beckett. Have you had zero sensitivity training? What in the world are my family's generous annual donations to HabSec being used for?"

I looked Varsity square in his dull, narrow eyes for one long moment I held his gaze until his face turned a blotchy shade of red and he suddenly became interested in the walkway.

"Yeah, okay." He tried to brush it off, but the tough-guy posturing had been thoroughly skewered. He ran a scarred hand through close-cropped sandy blonde hair.

"I tell you what, Marrow. The fiancé says you were the last person to see Rocket alive. So you take a few to process your grief or whatever, but I want your butt in a chair at the station giving us a statement within the next twenty-four hours. After that, I'm putting out a public notice that you're wanted for questioning as a person of interest in a murder investigation. That sensitive enough for you?"

I stepped into the house and slammed the door in his face without another backward glance.

The foyer was empty. The godawful yellow marble floor was immaculately clean and newly polished, shining like a well-preserved mustard stain. If I'm being honest, I had expected a lot more . . . dead brother to be there. It hadn't been long enough for Health Services to collect a body *and* for HabSec to run the full crime scene and clean up after. I breathed in the synthetic white sage floor cleaner, and for a moment, I held on to the idea that perhaps Rocket wasn't dead. Maybe the whole thing had been a sick joke after all.

Then Disco peeked around the corner. His eyes were doubly lined: once with a thick application of metallic gold liner, and once more with the puffy red shade of a broken heart. I swallowed hard and opened my mouth to say something, anything, but instead of 'hi' or 'how are you,' all that came out was a warbled, inarticulate, strangely guttural cry.

He blinked at me in quiet surprise and said softly, "Wow. You changed into mourning clothes before coming over; I can't believe I didn't think of that. I should change, too—"

I looked down at my black heels, black tights, black sharkskin skirt, black bra top, and shook my head. "Disco, it's me. Relax. This is my normal."

"Huh." He let out a trilling laugh that echoed garishly around us. "Yeah, I guess it is."

My brother's fiancé looked at me and then looked down to the floor. I paused for a long moment to give him room to explain. At last as my mouth began to form a question, Disco suddenly reanimated, his eyes looking up wide and watery. He didn't say a word, but instead made a small, anguished squeal in the back of his throat and came running out on razor-thin stiletto heels to throw his lanky arms around me in a tight hug.

Disco Bishop was the kind of old-fashioned clothing model with a build that some called slender and others called wraithlike, but you wouldn't know it by the way he hugged. Drowning men hugged life rafts with less enthusiasm.

"I didn't call HabSec, Marrow, I *swear*. I would never. *Or* Health Services! They just... showed up right after I called you!"

"Easy, Disco, I believe you"

He pulled away, and my gaze followed his down to the pristine floor where Rocket's body should have been. At the very least, there should have been blood spatters, outline tape, *something*.

"Call me crazy, but I thought you said Rocket died right here, Disco," I said gently as I could.

He flinched, crossing his arms defensively around his chest and hugging his shoulders.

"Varsity called it in as soon as he arrived. He took a 3D scan of the scene and some samples. Bots cleaned up the ... bots cleaned the floor. Your parents," he added, seeing the question forming on my face.

Of fucking course. Mom and Dad Nightingale would have demanded the height of discretion and a quick clean-up as soon as they had received word. *Hide the bodies first, get drunk and yell about it afterward when the cameras weren't watching* was practically the family motto.

But it did put a damper on the plans already marinating in my brain about how to get to the bottom of Rocket's sudden demise. Health Services would have taken Rocket deep into that bastion of red tape otherwise known as Electric Blue Moon General Hospital. As charming and generous with bribes as I was, it still wouldn't be easy for me to gain access.

I cast around, desperate for any trace of a clue. In the absence of a body, of any sort of blood or gore or scrap of fabric would suffice. I felt a scream rise up from deep in my gut, and I pushed the tip of my tongue to the roof of my mouth to keep it from escaping.

Disco, maybe sensing my distress or maybe just looking for something to do with himself, ducked into the adjoining den as I prowled the foyer and returned bearing two Mai Tais in crystal glasses appropriately shaped like skulls. Each was garnished with a wedge of blackened pineapple and a tiny black umbrella. The effect was a little old-fashioned, but it was a classic mourning drink.

Tears edged along the corners of my eyes and blinked them away, accepting the cup with a nod of thanks. This was the sort of cocktail you drank standing around at your great uncle's funeral. I downed half of mine in one go and reeled from the cloying sweetness. It tasted remarkably like bile.

"How strong did you make these?" I coughed.

"I used surface-proof rums . . . three different kinds I found in the back of the liquor cabinet." He had the decency to blush. Surface-proof booze was wickedly potent and not something you sprang on someone without a warning. "Do you want something lighter?"

I waved off Disco's question and set the drink on the entry side table.

"Walk me through what I happened," I urged him instead.

"Well, um, so I was out for the day, doing a gig at the Liu Komen Spring-Summer show. We had a *ridiculously* early call time so I left the house this morning around four a.m. But worth it, you know, because there were so many A-listers in the audience, and *FashHags* and *Splashion* both did vid segments on the show. After, I went out to tea with Kitten, Péri, and Tang. Péri was being *such* a cob nobbler the entire time and was like 'why are we getting tea when pizza exists?' and it's like because some of us have actual meal plans we'd like to not fuck up? And that took a few hours because Tang's been going through some shit—*you* probably know all about that—but when we parted ways I realized I left my favorite tote at the workout studio so I took a little detour—"

I cut him off, pinching the bridge of my nose. "When you got *home*, Disco. Walk me through what happened when you got home. When did you find Rocket?"

Disco nodded. "Oh, right, yeah, of course. Well I got home around five, I suppose, and oh God, Marrow, I practically tripped over his body. Then, well I lost my mind a bit, screaming and everything. I checked to see if maybe he was still alive, which of course he wasn't with that gaping hole in the back of his head and his brains all over the walls and floor like that. And then…"

When he didn't continue I prompted, "Then?"

"Then I called you. And then I called your parents, you know," Disco rushed to add. "I figured they should hear it from family rather than HabSec or the news or something.. Then the ambulance showed up. Along with HabSec."

It was nothing at all to go on. I ran my hands through my hair, thinking. "Disco, think carefully, alright? You said there was blood, and Rocket, was there *anything* else out of place? Anything missing from the house? Were there signs of a struggle?" I looked at the walls. There wasn't so much as a scratch on them, but Disco had said Rocket had a hole in his head. "A bullet casing, maybe?"

Before he could answer, my com buzzed and I checked it on reflex. It was a text from a local habitat news channel asking for some interview time with the bereaved family. I shook my head and looked up in time to see Disco glance at his own com.

"It's Channel Three," he said. I showed him my screen. "VBC here."

"Ugh, can't they leave us alone for two seconds?"

I put my com on Do Not Disturb and tried to turn Disco's attention back to the matter at hand.

"I should call Mom and Dad, too. Check in. What did they say when you talked to them?"

He shrugged nervously and ran pale fingers through thick, kelp-green hair.

"They were upset, you know? Told me to keep it quiet. Said Nightingales handled their own affairs on their own terms, and they didn't want any publicity. Said they'd be headed back to Electric Blue Moon just as soon as Kline was done getting some deal signed."

I picked up my drink and frowned into it. Figures Dad wouldn't want a little speed-bump like the death of his only son to come between him and a multi-billion doubloon business merger. I felt the tears coming on again, but they weren't the sad kind. I pushed them back down with a sip of Mai Tai.

"Disco—I know this sounds ridiculous—but can you think of anyone who had it out for Rocket?"

I sure as fuck couldn't. Even my brother's rivals loved him. He was just that kind of guy. Those who crossed him felt honored to have even held his attention long enough for him to crush them. I used to tease him that he was too pretty to hate. It was no surprise when Disco shook his head, but then he hesitated.

"Except . . ."

"Except?" I prompted.

"Well, you know about the trip he took out to Gucci's pleasure cabin last weekend, right?" He glanced nervously at me and I licked the inside of my teeth with the tip of my tongue.

Gucci Merriweather was Rocket's lifelong best friend and Electric Blue Moon's playboy extraordinaire. He was also so hot he could have set every topside continent ablaze with a glance, if they hadn't already been on fire for two decades running. The boy had a voice like molten steel and strong, nimble hands that came equipped with an intimate map of every body's pleasure triggers. We were familiar—to put it lightly—and I had known about the little getaway they'd taken with a dozen or so of their closest friends, though I hadn't gone with them, for reasons Disco knew.

"Yeah, I heard something about it," I hedged, waiting to see where this was going.

"Oh that was right around the time you were tracking down Velour Jameson and her new joyfriend, wasn't it?" I nodded and he shrugged. "I couldn't go, either. I had a gig. Anyway, Rocket came back pissed. Like, *really* pissed. He'd gotten into it with someone there, but he wouldn't tell me who or about what. He just changed into his workout clothes and went out to run stairs."

Rocket only did cardio when he was too angry to do drugs.

"Wow, he *was* pissed."

"Right? Anyway, he wasn't the same after that. I never did find out what that was all about." He blinked and choked out a sob. "I guess I won't ever now that he's . . ."

Disco covered his mouth with one hand and pressed his back to the wall, as if he needed it to keep him upright. His knees and shoulders shook as grief overtook him. I closed the distance between us and awkwardly put an arm around his shoulder, but I was worthless for comfort beyond that.

While Disco wept, I scanned the room again. There had been a rug in their foyer; a green shag monstrosity that threatened to devour high heels and bare toes alike. It, too, was gone. Either boxed up for evidence at HabSec's central offices or, more likely given their incompetence, incinerated in the cleaning bot's attempts to scrub away the gore.

I slipped away from Disco and shifted the entryway table a few inches to the side, exposing a thin layer of undisturbed dust in the space between it and the wall. It hadn't been disturbed during whatever had taken place. The foyer was only ten feet wide; it was possible that if Rocket had wrestled with his assailant they would have missed the table entirely, but it wasn't likely. I sensed he had known his killer, perhaps had even invited them inside and thus prevented the security cams outside from picking up anything unusual. If they had captured the murder on screen, Varsity wouldn't be lurking outside.

Disco's voice pulled me from my thoughts. "You should talk to Gucci," he sniffled, "he would know what Rocket's mood was about for sure."

Disco put a hand on my shoulder and fixed me with a well-practiced beseeching gaze. "Marrow . . . you and I both know HabSec is a total joke. But you're the real deal. Nightingale Detective Agency is where everyone goes when they want hard answers. And it's Rocket we're talking about. You're on the case, aren't you?"

Every shred of common sense and instinct said I shouldn't. I was too close to the victim. I was the one who would inherit his part of the family fortune now that he was gone. Anyone in law enforcement would look at my involvement and see a guilty woman trying to muddy the waters—cover her tracks. And beyond all of that, our parents would do all they could to ice me out of the details. But I couldn't just stand around while HabSec bungled their way through the case, either. I needed answers. I needed to get out of that fucking foyer.

I polished off my Mai Tai.

"You're damn right I am. Look, I've got to go. Varsity's lurking on me and I'm overdue for a shower. Don't talk to the press, Disco. I'll be in touch."

I slipped out the back and headed home on foot via the most unlikely and inconvenient route possible in order to avoid both HabSec and the press. Three hundred meters below the surface, we didn't have stars or a moon to gaze up at on lonesome nights like they do in the old movies, but an obliging school of blue lanternfish swept over the transparent hab roof just as I happened to glance up. I remembered how as a child, Rocket used to drop everything and gawp upward at them as though they were made of pure magic. The soft pulsing glow of the school swirled in on itself before the lead lantern picked a direction and they swam in an arc to some unknown destination in the great beyond. Once the last fish disappeared into the dark, the tears started and they didn't stop until long after I'd made it home.

It was nearly seven in the morning when I finally splashed some water on my face, took a few aspirin, settled a big hat over my red-rimmed eyes, and headed over to Gucci's townhouse. It wasn't far from my place, and since the newshounds weren't expecting me to emerge before the fashionable hour of one in the afternoon, I was able to slip out with a group of neighbors leaving for work and avoid their face-recognition drones altogether.

In my line of work, I had to get pretty chummy with the press, I knew some of them staked out on my street on a first-name basis. They wouldn't be too happy with the hat trick I'd just pulled; I made a mental note to offer an exclusive interview to whomever I'd need the biggest favor from later on down the line.

When I got to Gucci's, the circular windows in all three stories spilled pools of strobing rainbow light onto the sidewalk and bass thrummed heavily out from the walls, reverberating in my chest. I couldn't be sure if I was arriving at the tail end of one party or the beginning of another.

Gucci himself answered the door when I rang the bell, clad only in a perfect smile and a dozen tattoos over honey-toned skin. His shaggy black hair was artfully tousled and he did not waste the opportunity to brush it slowly out of his eyes with fanned fingers. Animated black hearts grew until they burst like fireworks on every OLED-tipped fingernail.

"Marrow!" His expression turned quickly from curiosity to delighted surprise.

"Gucci Merriweather," I forced my voice to rise above the music, barely.

"Baby, baby, I am so sorry for your loss," Gucci rumbled, ushering me inside. He wrapped his arms around my shoulders so tenderly that I felt spooked. This flavor of kindness, from him of all people, didn't sit well in my stomach. I let him hug me for one beat, two, then pulled away and brushed glitter out of his trim black goatee to give my hands something to do.

"It's hard on all of us, I'm sure. Thanks."

All of us, I'd said. As though I actually counted among Gucci and Rocket's set. As though there was any reality where I was meant to be standing in a home designed for the world's richest, getting hugged by a man whose veins practically bled gold.

The truth was, I was a Surfacer garment-girl's spawn. A fortunate orphan of an unfortunate accident. Plucked by the hand of fate known as Carmen Nightingale to be her salvation from bad publicity. My birth parents—and by proxy my four-year-old self—had come to the hab on a work visa; my mother and father both working in-house for the Nightingales. When careless work conditions—an equipment malfunction, they'd called it—snuffed them both out before their time, the press eagerly waited to see what would become of me. Would I be heartlessly deported topside? Conveniently shipped off to a different hab? Every way forward looked damning to the Nightingale name. All ways except one.

Lucky for me, I was a cute kid, and clever. I shudder to think what excuses they would have made if I'd been deemed too ugly or stupid. But I mugged well for the cameras and was endlessly quotable in the way precocious kids can be, and so I had been adopted into the family that got both my birth parents killed. I was brought up alongside the scions of Electric Blue Moon since we were old enough to read. None of them ever let me forget that I hadn't done anything special to be admitted into their world, that I didn't truly belong. But on paper, at least, I was Rocket's little sister and that made me good enough to be seen with. Good enough to fuck. And now, good enough to mourn beside.

Gucci let a few tears blur his mascara as he led me deeper into his home.

"I'm sorry," he said, fanning his face. "It's just still so much to process, you know? Of course you know, look who I'm asking. I'm just so glad you could make it to our little wake."

A wake, huh? From where I stood, it looked more like Gucci's social life on any day ending in a "y."

"So when was the last time you spoke to Rocket?"

Gucci did a double-take and looked me over with a new, sharper light in his eyes.

"I know that tone. That's your Marrow Nightingale, detective-at-large, you-got-five-seconds-before-I-drag-you -into-a-dark-alley tone. You're working your own brother's case? Have you lost your sexy damned mind?"

"Just answer the question, Gucci."

"Well, quite a lot, I guess. He's been staying here for a few weeks now."

That was news. I raised an eyebrow.

"He was staying with you? Why?"

Gucci kept talking at me over his shoulder as I followed him into the kitchen.

"You want some . . ." Gucci gestured with one hand to the kitchen counters. Every available space was buried in to-go containers, half-empty bottles of booze and mixers, abandoned plates, abandoned cups, and a dizzying assortment of unattended delicacies slowly spoiling. "Sustenance? We've got kelpburgers, mint ice cream burritos, spicy caramel soup, rainbow coconut fried rice, pistachio curd pizza, the *best* banana pudding, sushi—*lots* of sushi here . . ."

"I'm not hungry. And you know I hate sushi," I cut him off before he could finish taking inventory. "What do you mean you have banana pudding? Bananas haven't existed for like, thirty years, Gucci."

Nothing in the piles of food remotely resembled pudding or bananas.

Gucci giggled the laugh of the incredibly high and shrugged and we passed through the kitchen and the dining room to his cavernous living room. "That's what it says on the container, anyway. But come on. If you're not hungry, let's get you a proper drink." He paused to consider his words. "Is it the breakfast hour yet?"

"You're avoiding my questions, but I'll take that drink. What was Rocket doing couch-surfing with you when his wedding was three months away?"

In the dim, smoky living room, Gucci only shrugged wiry shoulders and set to work at the bar, leaving me momentarily to my own devices. There were a dozen or so guests sprawled out over a lounge of plush pillows and faux fur blankets, all in various states of undress. I watched Gucci from the corner of my eye as he picked up first a gin bottle then the absinthe, but my attention was pulled away when a burnished brown arm tipped with lasciviously pink fingernails shot up from the sweaty pile of limbs and waved at me.

"Koko?" I asked, carefully stepping over and around the mourners to reach the man attached to the arm. Kokomo

Prince sat up and beamed a broad, languid smile in my direction.

Koko had been crying recently, that much I could tell from the puffy redness around his warmed-whiskey eyes, but he had buried the more immediate pain of Rocket's loss deep under layers of drugs and diversions of the flesh.

"Marrow, baby, you didn't tell me you would be dropping by this little soirée! I would have called and coordinated sex toys with you."

He held up a glittery orange dildo and giggled.

"Wasn't invited." Not that I would have joined in, regardless. A murdered brother isn't what I'd call the best aphrodisiac.

"Yes you were," Gucci sang out over his shoulder. He pivoted away from the bar and pouted towards me, drink outstretched. I accepted the Sea Devil—that's seaweed gin and absinthe mixed over sugared ice and shot through with cloudy tendrils of squid ink bitters—and frowned.

"Was I?"

"Do you *ever* check your messages, baby?"

I glanced at my com screen and flinched. Forty-nine unread messages since last night.

"Been too busy being sad, I guess. Cheers. To Rocket," I held up my glass and clinked with Gucci's. Koko cheekily donked his dildo against our cups before he was pulled back into the cuddle puddle by impatient paramours.

"Make yourself at home, all right?" Gucci said to me.

"Yeah but Gucci, why was Rocket—"

The doorbell buzzed over the music, cutting me off, and Gucci sashayed toward the front of the house to play host.

I sipped my cocktail as I glanced around at the heavily occupied floor. I had come to blend in and ask questions, but the crowd at Gucci's didn't seem down for the sort of conversation I had in mind. I'd have to get my answers some other way. Armed with the recent but vague information that Rocket had been crashing at Gucci's town-house, I left the living room and wandered down the halls searching for Rocket's guest room.

It wasn't until a little green-skinned girl with spiky rainbow hair and silver hooves for feet tapped me on the leg and handed me a holographic, Curaçao-blue business card before melting into the floor that I realized Gucci had slipped me something in my drink. What the fuck.

I stared at the unblemished spot of carpet where the green girl had been, then squinted furiously at the card until the letters stopped blurring and arranged them-selves into something that made sense. It was a calling card for the Kraken Club, a burlesque and cocktails joint located in the Steam District, tucked discretely beneath the mechanical operations decks in a muggy, remote sec-tor of the hab. One side was a little holographic image of their current star, Lexi Lagoon, a real honest-to-God mermaid. Her tail and hair moved subtly with every twitch of the card, her illustrated breasts rising and fall-ing with stylized excitement. I flipped it over and found a hand-written note scrawled across the back:

Dear Rocket: A pleasure doing business with you as always, stud. Stop by any time for a friendly drink—on the house.

It was signed with a perfect, iridescent green lipstick kiss. I waited for the lips to turn into a talking fish or a robot or some other conjuring of my drug-addled con-sciousness, but when they remained lips I had to wonder: what sort of business did Rocket have with Lexi Lagoon?

The man took the words *family legacy* to heart like a mantra. Sure, he liked to have as much fun as anybody, but his business decisions were always textbook perfect. Rocket lived every day in public as though he were sitting at the front of a class, watching his posthumous biography. His reputation was spotless.

Lexi, on the other hand, had arrived at the hab in the dead of night and a maelstrom of gossip had followed. Mermaids weren't naturally born, they were corporate property, created deep in the bowels of Sealliance' labs. Hard to imagine Rocket would risk the ire of the biggest megacorp in the solar system for a business investment with a rogue android.

I pocketed the card and kept searching, but Gucci's surprise ingredient was aggressive and soon my world was nothing but glitter and wool. I made my way back to the living room, crawled into an armchair, and let the cocktail do its work.

The sudden absence of light and music eventually brought me back to my senses. There were impatient groans all around me, and then the power flickered back on.

"Another fucking blackout?" someone mumbled into my elbow. "That's the third one this week."

I found myself snuggled between the speaker, cocooned inside a rainbow-fur blanket, and a woman on my left who rested her pink-haired head on my shoulder and softly murmured lines of poetry to herself. I waited for a pause and then I smiled and gently extricated myself from their warmth and fuzzy awareness. It was late—much later than I had intended on staying—and as I fumbled for my com, I found I still had no messages from my parents or the morgue.

"Koko?" I looked around but saw no trace of him. He was either in one of the more private orgy rooms or already gone. "Gucci?"

I heard a shriek of laughter from the kitchen and headed in that direction. Gucci was there with two others I didn't know. His friends smiled at me with visible disinterest.

"Gucci, you son of a bitch," I said. I'd have punched him, but my fingers were still numb and my vision swam. "You drugged me? Really? What the fuck was in that?"

His eyes went wide, like he was dealing with an upset puppy.

"Baby, I thought you'd want something extra! That was from my personal stash—the designer shit, you know? You've been perfectly safe. A few hours of R & R is what our Rocky would have wanted for you."

He leaned in for a parting hug and I pushed him away, using the proximity to look him hard in the eyes. I knit my eyebrows together, letting my lips fall back in just enough of a snarl to show the tips of my teeth, and let the look sink in. He was a sucker for a dramatic pause and flagrant displays of emotion. I put both to work.

"You are *not* forgiven. I'll get back to you when I think of a way for you to make it up to me. I've got somewhere to be." I turned to leave but paused in the doorway. I wanted to storm out, but I couldn't leave without the information I'd come for. I glanced back at Gucci's contrite face over my shoulder. "Before I go, I still need to know a few things. What were Disco and Rocket fighting about? Why did he come back from your weekend getaway mad? Why was he staying with you?"

I turned back to face him, arms crossed over my chest. Gucci gave the other two a significant look until they picked up their drinks and obediently left the room. Then he leaned in and spoke to me in a gossip's whisper.

"A couple of weeks ago, Campari Westwood threatened to expose Disco. Rocky offered to give Disco some space, suggested they put the wedding plans on hold until Westwood found fresher prey, but Disco accused Rocky of trying to distance himself from their engagement to save his own reputation. He lost his mind over it a bit and told him to find another bed. So, Rocky came here, of course."

Oh, damn. Campari Westwood was the tabloid queen of not just Electric Blue Moon, but of all the habs in the Pacific. Her news org, *The Conch*, was everywhere: at everyone's fingertips, in every public space. Like a norovirus. If Campari wanted a hot rumor could become a hard fact before it had time to lose the boozy scent of the breath that whispered it.

That *The Conch* would go after a couple as high-profile as Disco and Rocket was itself not surprising. Westwood's column goblins ran a new unsubstantiated rumor about the Nightingale family every few months as a matter of business. What was surprising was that this time her threats had caused a rift between the inseparable couple. Disco and Rocket had always shown a united front against the press.

"Expose Disco over what?" I asked and Gucci shrugged.

"Shiny new drugs? An affair? Raw footage of a bad hair day? Who knows, right? Campari's always got something, baby, you know that. Rocket wouldn't tell me much. Just that Disco was pissed at Campari *and* at Rocket for not doing enough to protect him from her. Whatever *It* is, Campari's holding off on the story for now. Murder makes for better press, so she got the clicks she was after in the end, I suppose" he added bitterly.

Despite spending the entire day in a stupor, I was suddenly very tired. I rubbed my eyes and headed for the door.

"Take care of yourself, Gucci," I said over my shoulder. "And fuck you."

"Mea culpa, my darling Nightingale! I'll make it up to you somehow. Stay out of trouble," he added. "Go mourn like a normal person and leave this case to HabSec!"

I flipped him off as I walked down the steps. Leave it to HabSec, sure. I'd let those clowns handle my brother's murder the day I grew gills.

✳

I left Gucci's with two new leads and a strong hunger for Infinity's coconut shrimp plate Plus, I still owed Infinity my tab from the night before. I'd lost a lot of time thanks to Gucci's surprise cocktail—it was already after eight— and as I stepped through the diffused rainbow glow of the doors to the bar, I was greeted by somber raised glasses from the regulars lined up on their barstools. Everyone had heard the news about Rocket. I made my way to the small, tucked-away red vinyl booth I referred to only half-jokingly as my "office." I had handled a lot of cases from that cozy banquette, but this evening it was a slice of companionable solitude.

I tried to call my parents again and got sent straight to voicemail for my trouble. The morgue's number didn't even give me that much dignity and rang for three solid minutes before I hung up.

"This one's on the house, Mare," Infinity came by and set a black umbrella-garnished Mai Tai on a coaster. "Sorry for your loss. Rocket was a top notch guy."

I looked away, unable to meet his eyes. "Yeah. He was one of the best of us. Thanks, Fin. I appreciate the thought."

The bar was quickly filling up with the post-workday rank-and-file, so Infinity gave me a parting nod of comfort and went back to his post. I took a few sips of my drink, rolling the deep, complex flavors of rum, citrus, and almond over my tongue, and people-watched. Infinity had used his best rums—hab-strength, thankfully—and elevated them with the perfect amount of orgeat, but it wasn't enough to quell the nauseating hollowness eating away at my gut.Absently, I quaffed the rest of my drink as I tried my parents' numbers. No answer anywhere, no texts or voicemails waiting for me. As much as I moaned about needing my space, I wasn't used to being this alone, unmoored. My mind was as restless as my stomach. I tried to settle the stormy tides inside myself with a few puffs from a vape pen and, suspecting that wouldn't be enough to do the trick, I fished a couple of happy caterpillars out of the bottom of my bag. In retrospect, I probably should have waited for the shrimp plate to arrive before finishing the drink, or at least held off on the little green pills.

Next thing I knew, the food still hadn't arrived and I was swaying in my booth with a woolly brain and numb hands, watching the crowd swell into every nook and cranny. The DJ turned up the music to match the constant current of chatter and shouted greetings, and the sound washed over me like I had physically submerged myself in it. I was drenched in the noise and wishing it would drown me. That was when Campari Westwood showed up.

As cool as I could, I flipped up my compact mirror and applied a fresh coat of lipstick—a dark and wicked velvet matte red. The caterpillars kept my hands from shaking, at least. The standing-room crowd around the bar parted for Campari's entourage like a school of fish makes room for a tiger shark.

Campari's top section editors, Gwynetha and Kitten, flanked her like a pair of stylized eels. They wore sleek black suits that played a stream of *The Conch*'s latest headlines in real time along their backs and thighs. Their shrapnel-lined, neon eyes studied the room. Always on the hunt for the next story. Kitten made eye contact and the happy caterpillars marched down the nerves along my spine, making my smile reckless, my temper bold. I kept eye contact until he looked away, then I got up and made my way to the bar for a fresh drink. By the time I got there, one stool down from their boss, her news goons were right at my elbow.

"Doesn't Campari ever give you two the night off?" I asked, keeping my eyes fixed on the bottles lining the back of the bar.

Campari and I were the same age, had attended the same education pods, ran around in the same crowd almost our entire lives. She loved direct attention more than anything, and she hated it when someone spoke to her without looking at her. And she *really* hated it when people spoke about her as though she wasn't right there in the room. As expected, she took the bait.

"I'm surprised to see you here, Nightingale," Campari purred. "Word has it the first thing you did when informed of your foster-brother's untimely death was to head straight to an orgy. A little gauche, in my opinion. And now here you are, drinking alone at a bar? Care to comment?"

I flagged down Infinity for a double gin on the rocks. Without looking at anyone I asked, "You ever had Infinity's seaweed gin? He distills it right here in the back of the house. Nothing else like it."

Campari ignored the question. She leaned in closer to hiss in my ear. "Some say you haven't been seen shedding a single tear for Rocket. That you've been on a celebratory bender since you saw the corpse. Not really the behavior of a loving sister who just lost her big brother, is it? Tell me, how much is Disco Bishop paying you for your part in all this? Did he act alone, or were you an *eager* little angler to help him pull the trigger?"

Ah, so she assumed Disco was the culprit *and* believed I had been there when the body was found. Interesting. I sipped my gin slowly. The bittersweet herbs hit cold and sharp on my tongue, pressing the fury I felt down between my teeth. It splintered in my mouth like shards of ice.

"Did *you* mop up the blood? That was sort of your birth mom's whole thing, wasn't it? Cleaning up inconvenient messes?" Campari leaned in close so that only I could hear her. "We both know a castaway rag like you would do anything to keep her paws on a lifestyle she never should have had in the first place. Did the Nightingales finally get tired of footing the bill for their charity case? A creature like you would do anything to avoid surface deportation, wouldn't you? What's Disco paying you to cover for him?"

Everything caught up to me all at once. The sleep deprivation, the drugs. Anger, insult, grief, and the unslaked thirst of a murder investigation roiled in my booze-brined gut. It wasn't a part of my plan to get physical, but I was dangling over an abyss inside and at that moment, I couldn't see any other way but down.

I tossed the rest of my drink back and set the glass carefully on the bar. Campari was still smirking at my ear. In one swift move, I brought a right hook up to meet her chiseled chin. She stumbled back against the bar, splashing something bright green along the sleeve of her jacket and her eyes went wide with shock before the pain even registered. Then my knee found Campari's stomach and she collapsed to the ground in a satisfying heap. Or it would have been satisfying, if I hadn't realized at that exact moment how contrived the fall was, how she didn't even try to defend herself, how a lot of people were screaming in alarm but even more were filming the mess with their coms. Goddamnit.

A big pair of hands grabbed me roughly from behind and spun me around so fast that my drug-loosened legs tangled and I dropped in an ungainly heap on the ground. It was Varsity, of all people, because of course. Of course Campari would show up at the bar where everyone knew to find me. Of course she would have notified HabSec of a possible security threat on the premises in advance. Campari had baited me with the oldest trick in the book, and I'd grabbed her line like a starving dumbass mola mola fish.

Kitten and Gwynetha helped Campari to her feet, murmuring soft exclamations of concern. She wiped blood from her mouth with the back of her hand, making sure her on-scene photographers got a few good snaps of it in the process.

"You might carry the Nightingale name for now, but everyone knows exactly what you are and where you belong. You're done in Electric Blue Moon. Send us a postcard from whatever's left of Los Angeles when you get there, Marrow."

"Let's go, *detective*," Varsity hauled me up and shoved me towards the exit. "After we get you booked for this altercation, you and I can have that little chat about your whereabouts on the night of your brother's death."

Rocket was only a year older than me. Twenty-five to my twenty-four. Two decades as siblings: laughing, fighting, scheming against our tutors, supporting each other through love interests and heartbreak and rivalries, cheering on victories—well, Rocket usually was the one with the victories. I was forever the black sheep, the charity case, the one our parents brought along on social outings "so she'll learn how to fit in."

Did I want to fit in? I don't know. I was just a kid with rapidly dwindling memories of the family who had accepted me the way I was and the glamorous Nightingales were my whole world. I suddenly had new clothes every year, a hair stylist who knew me by name before I was six, a bedroom bigger than our old shabby apartment, all to myself. After that accident, I never wanted for anything again, and that was nice. But I had always had an ornery streak. Hearing the polite distance in tone from my foster parents' mouths made me dream of swimming up to the surface and never looking back.

But no matter how out of place I felt, Rocket had always, no matter what, been my brother. He had taught me how to swim in a mersuit, how to play squid poker, how to stick up for myself. The first time he found me alone, holed up in the den in front of a screen, he had asked me why I wasn't ready to go. We were sixteen and there was a birthday party that night for a kid from our same tutoring pod. Go to what, I asked? They'd sent the invitation addressed to Rocket only. I thought he was going to drag me out with him. Instead, he left the room, came back a few minutes later with a carton of ice cream and two spoons and told me to quit hogging the couch. After that, everyone knew the Nightingale siblings were a team.

We grew into our independent lives as we grew up, as all siblings do, but I never doubted for a moment that Rocket would have my back if I needed him and he knew he could count on me for anything. Or at least, I liked to believe he knew that. I had to get my keel evened if I wanted to bring Rocket's killer to justice. No more distractions, no more staring into the abyss.

The door to the HabSec interrogation room slammed open, interrupting my navel-gazing. Varsity Beckett stepped inside and dropped into the chair across from me at the table. He had a datapad in one hand and a coffee cup in the other.

"Barroom brawls now, Marrow? Are you kidding me with this shit? What are your parents going to say when they see *that* on the feeds tonight?"

Varsity slurped his coffee and raised his eyebrows expectantly at me from the other side of the metal interrogation table. We couldn't save the planet, but somehow our horticulturists were able to grow actual arabica miles below the surface. Would wonders never cease.

"Hmm, what *would* Mom and Dad say? I don't know, they'd probably say something like, 'Well, at least she didn't become an ass-sniffing HabSec flunky.'"

It was deeply satisfying to watch that smirk drop into a scowl. I folded my arms over my chest and glared at the clock. Varsity had taken his time filling out the complaint paperwork before coming in to take my statement. It was nearly midnight. "How long are you going to keep me here, Varsity? Nothing better to do? There's a killer on the loose in the hab in case you hadn't heard."

"Funny, there haven't been any new murders reported since I scraped you off of the floor at Infinity's."

"You were *literally* there when I showed up at Rocket's house yesterday. *How* are you still pinning his death on me? Weren't you there to pick up clues, or something? Did you try checking the security feeds outside?"

"Let's talk about clues, Marrow." Varsity sat forward and turned on his recording tablet. "How many did *you* find staggering from one bottle to the next?"

A few, actually, but I didn't need him knowing about them. I raised an eyebrow at the recorder and shook my head.

"I just lost my only sibling. I comforted his fiancé, then went to a wake at his best friend's house. Then I went to Infinity's Cup when—"

"When you got shit-faced and punched the most powerful person in the gossip industry in front of a dozen hot coms. Yeah. We've got that part covered." Varsity shook his head in what seemed to be sincere disbelief, which somehow made it far worse than when he was being a sarcastic piece of shit. He looked at me again, more serious this time. "What the hell came over you, Nightingale?"

"Grief's a weird and unpredictable mistress," I shrugged. "Well, you've got my statement on both events and you've got five minutes left to charge me with something before you can no longer detain me so... what's it going to be, Varsity? One of us has a murder to solve."

Varsity sighed, switched off the recorder, and sent over a meeting date for the next week to my com. "Westwood's pressing charges, obviously. Here's your court date. You're free to go but if you so much as get caught littering, HabSec is legally obligated to remove you from Electric Blue Moon for the continued safety and well-being of our citizens."

I gathered my things and flipped him off. He stood up, blocking my path to the door.

"I'm talking surface deportation, Marrow."

"Heard you the first time, officer."

He stood there for a long moment, his self-righteous eyes boring into my best impression of a sullen rich-kid, then made a noise of disgust in the back of his throat and stepped aside.

"Get the fuck out of here. And stay out of my way," he growled.

"Funny, I was just about to tell you the same thing."

"The Nightingales aren't going to save you this time. Not if you had a hand in the death of their only son. And I shouldn't have to explain it to you, but interfering with an ongoing murder investigation is *also* grounds for deportation."

I was too tired for another round of snappy comebacks. I found Koko waiting for me in the HabSec lobby, making small talk with the desk clerk. When he saw me, he presented me with a hot cup of coffee and a knowing smirk.

"You are my personal savior," I said after a grateful sip. "Tell me you haven't been waiting here this entire time."

Koko laughed and shook his head, "Marrow I love you, but not *that* much. I was already out when I saw your face all over the feeds. Varsity always keeps people he hates up to the last minute so . . ." he shrugged expansively, "I figured midnight would be the magic hour to come pick you up. Someone's got to look out for you, baby. You're certainly not looking after yourself." He walked me out of the station and when we were around the corner he stopped and wordlessly held his arms open.

I wasn't done being angry about the situation. I wasn't done being scared for myself, either. But Koko's eyes were filled with infinite, tender love and kindness and I remembered that he had just lost a dear friend, too, and I hadn't stopped to ask him how he was holding up. And there he was, my neon fur-clad angel coming to my rescue bearing coffee. Tears threatened to spill over my cheeks. I stepped into Koko's arms and hugged him as tightly as I could.

"C'mon. You *cannot* sleep at your place tonight all by your little lonesome self. You're coming home with me and I don't want to hear any objections. You're already the top news story on *The Conch*, of course. If I let you out of my sight again, who knows what would happen, and I shall not be responsible for whatever that might be."

"Campari's pressing charges for assault. I think HabSec might be too scared of Nightingale influence and money to actually deport me but Koko, Varsity's got a raging hard-on to send me up the tube and *what if—*"

He cut me off with a brisk shush and another hug.

I drank my coffee and went back to Koko's place. We stayed up a little longer, talking quietly about Rocket. I filled Koko in on everything until, yawning, he confessed he had an early day in the morning and went to bed.

I needed the sleep, too, but I needed answers more. And a full day had been wasted between Gucci's party and my stint in HabSec's processing room. I didn't have the luxury of shut-eye, not when Rocket's killer was still out there somewhere. I lay on Koko's couch until I was certain he was asleep, then scribbled a note for him and quietly slipped out. It was only two in the morning. If I hurried, I could make it to the Kraken Club before last call.

✳

Every hab has its rhythms that it keeps to—the lights come on and turn off at set times in a twenty-four hour period, to mimic the night and day cycles happening on the surface. But in the big habs—the underwater metropolises like Electric Blue Moon—there are some parts that never truly sleep. Dark neighborhoods that thrive in the shadows created by the slick, shiny mountains of wealth and enterprise.

Such was the case with the Steam District—the collection of service alleys, worker's clubs, fly-by-night distilleries, and neon-scorched shop-fronts that catered to even the most eclectic Blue Moon vices. It was well past two in the morning by the time I got there, but the Smoke's doorways and streets still—well, if they didn't exactly *thrum* with life, there was still a restless heartbeat in the air.

The Kraken Club sat on the outer edge of the district, a single-story building sporting a new inky purple paint job, a red velvet rope, and a flashing sign that looked legitimately salvaged from a long-lost West Hollywood club. It wasn't so long ago that the Kraken had been an unremarkable pit stop for the illicit adventures of restless weekenders. That all changed when Lexi Lagoon made it her personal base of operations two months prior.

Here's a mystery for you: A lab-grown mermaid wearing the bloodless pearly face of a god, a tail like angel wings dripping sunrise, and a sugar-sweet mouth spitting frantic curses, shows up at Electric Blue Moon in the middle of the night. Her corporate logos have been scrubbed from her skin with highly caustic acid.

The mermaid is accompanied by an octopus, a stolen harpoon gun, and a small cargo hold filled to the brim with advanced surgical equipment. After a few whispers into the right ears—whose ears, exactly, I haven't been able to pin down—and none of this is remarked upon in the news feeds ever again. Not even in the gossip rags. Not even Campari touches the story.

Four weeks and a full building remodel later, Lexi was headlining at the Kraken Club as though she always had been, and suddenly the Kraken Club was the hottest venue in the hab.

The whole situation was fishy enough that I might have looked into it myself—if anyone had been interested in paying me to do so. Maybe while she was filling me in on my brother's final days, Lexi would be kind enough to divulge just how she ended up in the Steam District.

"Whoa, whoa, where do you think you're going?" The doorman, a hefty chunk of impatience and augmented muscle, held up a wide hand to block my entry. I gestured towards the door.

"Inside, preferably. I'd like to catch what's left of the last show." I pulled out my cred stick and locked on to the doorman's com with a three-digit doubloon offer. "It's been a long night, friendo. I just want to unwind. You get me?"

He glanced down at the amount displayed on his screen and snorted. I couldn't tell if I'd under or over-bribed, but he hit accept all the same and pulled open the door for me.

"Welcome to the Kraken Club."

I nodded my thanks and stepped past him into the muggy, vape-hazed interior. Even at such a late hour on a weekday, half of the tables were occupied along with most of the stools at the bar. I took a seat nearest the action at the front of the house and could see right away why Lexi was so popular.

The center stage of the club had been converted into a floor-to-ceiling aquarium, artfully lit to create a sea kingdom fantasia. An Atlantean myth interpreted through glitter and bioluminescent paint. A luxe clamshell bed, a few god-awful ornate gilt chairs, and a crystal chandelier evoked a shipwrecked palace fit for a queen. In the middle of all that was a gilded stripper pole which Lexi herself was putting to good use at that moment.

It wasn't just that she was beautiful, which she undoubtedly was, or that she was athletic enough to pull off unreal movements—she was a goddamned robot, after all. As the nu-candyhouse bass beat vibrated through my bones and Lexi artfully slipped out of her seashell bra to reveal a pair of iridescent puffy tits, she seduced the hab one customer at a time with our own founding mythos. Each curl of her veil-like tail, every delicate gesture of her fingers, her electric gaze shining out at us beneath extra-long lashes purred in so many electrified letters: *an underwater kingdom of lusty mermaids and bygone treasures can be yours! Just reach into the depths and take it, conqueror.*

Yet as I watched Lexi shimmy in a spotlight of glittery water, I couldn't see her coming between Rocket and Disco. She was larger than life up there and clearly in command of her own rising star. I tried to imagine what sort of business relationship the mermaid might have had with my brother and came up blank. Rocket was sexy and wealthy, sure, but there were so many bigger fish on Electric Blue Moon—no pun intended. Older, hornier fish with a lot more access and power. I'd been hired to catch plenty of them cheating on their spouses over the years; Lexi could have had half a dozen wrapped around that glorious tail. So what did Rocket have to do with any of this?

Lexi spun around the pole, fanning her tail wide, then swam in my direction. Her demeanor was lazily sensual, impersonal, but for a brief moment she looked directly into my eyes and nodded almost imperceptibly. Lexi flirtatiously blew a kiss in my direction and pirouetted off in a flurry of delicate pink, orange, and yellow fins to milk more doubloons out of her other patrons.

I might have thought I had imagined that knowing nod from her, but just then I felt the huge bouncer's hand land on my right shoulder.

"Lexi requests your presence backstage," he said in a low growl that hinted at what might happen were I to engage in any sort of funny business. I nodded, exhaled a cloud of vapor, and followed him through the club, down drab beige halls, where he left me alone in a humid dressing room.

It was posh and softly lit, furnished with a pair of red velvet lounge chairs and a cushioned bench for non-mermaids to sit. Along one wall stood a large plexiglass tub and, more conspicuously, a tall stack of crates marked with the Sealliance Tech Company logo. I trailed my fingers along the front of one crate, activating the small lock screen in the top center. It came to life with a small chime and the display panel requested I place my right-hand index and middle finger on the screen below. Biolocked, then.

Keyed to open only for a maximum of three individual sets of fingerprints, biolocks were an expensive and tedious way to secure anything, which is why they tended to only be used among the corporations for their most cutting-edge prototypes. Was this the rumored stolen medical equipment that Lexi had shown up with? Or was she dealing in something more? A dressing room seemed like hardly the place to stash goods that hot.

The full length of the back of the room was occupied by a large aquarium. Unlike the one out front, this one only came up to about chest height. The tank was done up with plush benches, cushions, and a floating table littered with pots of waterproof makeup and empty champagne bottles. Nearby, riveted to the wall safely above water level, was a secured computer console and a keyboard. A glittery rock rose out of the water close by, carved just right for classical mermaid lounging.

Alone, I took a seat in one of the chairs and waited for Lexi's performance to finish up. As I idly checked my com for messages, a slow movement in the tank caught my eye. I watched what had looked to be a red underwater cushion unfurl into the form of a red giant octopus. It blinked languidly as it regarded me.

"Hello, Ms. Nightingale," a distinctly robotic feminine-coded voice emitted from a speaker embedded in the wall near where I sat.

I jumped in my seat and the octopus continued to stare. Unsettling doesn't begin to describe that hyper-intelligent alien gaze, but I tried to keep it together.

"Are you . . . ?"

"Yes, I am an octopus. Yes, I am really talking to *you.* No, this is not a gimmick or a trick. My name is Charisma. A pleasure to meet you, detective."

"You're a talking octopus . . . stripper? What do you do, take off eight thigh-high stockings?"

Charisma stirred in a way that clearly telegraphed annoyance.

"First of all, it is called burlesque."

"So why aren't you out there on stage now?"

"And lower the price of exclusivity? I do one show a week with her, for a VIP list only. Do you have any idea, Ms. Nightingale, what those tickets sell for?"

Exclusive weird stuff was like candy-dipped drugs for the aristocrat set. The name of the game was to outdo all your friends in terms of kink and spectacle. No doubt the purchase of a single ticket to Lexi and Charisma's show could pay for a year of comfortable living on Electric Blue Moon.

A smattering of applause and a few wolf whistles from the front of the house indicated that Lexi's set had wrapped up. A moment later the mermaid herself swam through a discreet tunnel at the back of the tank.

"Ms. Nightingale," she said as she surfaced. Her voice sounded resonant, lyric. Like a human had had an auto-tune installed in their throat. I tried not to stare at the swell of her full, iridescent rainbow-painted lips or the water droplets that fell from the dark tips of her breasts. Whoever designed Lexi, I don't think their mind was one-hundred-percent focused on the subject of *marine* research. "Electric Blue Moon's famous private detective, in the flesh! They warned us when we set up shop that your curiosity would get the better of you and you'd be dropping by sooner or later. We were wondering how long it would take you. Would you care for a drink?"

I was also Electric Blue Moon's *only* private detective, but I didn't make a point of mentioning that.

"Ms. Lagoon." I nodded and cleared my throat. I wondered what else "they" had told the duo about me. "A drink would be swell, thanks."

She laughed and poured a glass of champagne. She glided over to the side of the tank to hand it to me. "Please, call me Lexi. Cheers."

"In that case, likewise. Call me Marrow. We can save the formalities for HabSec."

Charisma had moved closer, and I regarded her with slight unease as she appraised me with her large eyes.

"Marrow Nightingale," she said low and slow. Even through the robotic translator, she managed to sound sultry. "You're aptly named, baby. A dish like you, I could just suck you . . . right down to the bone."

Okay, sultry and more than a little unsettling. A red tentacle snaked up the side of the tank and I willed myself not to take a big step backward. The appendage morphed from red through blue to purple, pulsing suggestively.

"Are all octopuses such flatterers?" I asked.

"Only the ones who meet you, I suppose."

Lexi smirked and positioned herself elegantly atop her rock. Her gauzy tail fanned out delicately into the water, undulating slowly. I had no idea how to open a conversation with either a robotic mermaid or an octopus.

"Lexi, your tail, looks like a, what are they called, a betta fish. Did Sealliance build it that way, or is this a post-liberation mod?"

Lexi's laugh was low and sultry.

"An angel wing betta fish, yes, that's what my tail design was based off of. But mine's a little tougher than the real thing. Diamond nanoweave, like the outer hull of the habitats." She flexed her tail, and for a moment, the diaphanous main fin solidified into a razor sharp, deadly-looking serrated edge. Then she flexed it back and did a coy flick in the water.

I raised an eyebrow and took a sip of my drink. The champagne was excellent.

"Did you know that the betta fish's gorgeous plumage is only a trait of the male betta? I get compliments all the time about my glorious feminine fin but in reality, I am not just half-fish. half-android, but half-male. half-female. A merminx, I prefer to call myself."

I blushed. "Apologies on the pronouns, then."

Lexi waved a hand, laughing. "You didn't know. I've been trying to get them to change the sign out front since I got here, but it's tied up in fabrication."

Charisma wrapped an affectionate tentacle around Lexi's waist and Lexi reached down to boop Charisma's forehead with a finger.

"Anyway, Charisma here is the true gem. She's the real one of a kind, detective," Lexi declared proudly. "Thousands of my model toil diligently in every aquatic lab in every ocean."

"Is the pole-dancing routine factory standard?" I was pointedly ignored.

"Octopuses possess a level of dexterity that humans can only dream of, and with eight limbs, no less. Sealliance augmented her brainpower to rival that of their top neuroscientists. Who then oversaw her education as a surgeon."

"Ah, so you two met at work. You're a medical doctor, Charisma?"

"Not in the way they wanted me to be." Even the neutral artificial voice through the wall speaker couldn't mask the dryness in Charisma's tone.

"I take it those company crates weren't part of their standard severance package." I jerked a thumb towards the mystery stack.

The mention of the crates struck a nerve. The social levity evaporated in a slosh of tank water. Lexi said, "So what is it that we can do for you, detective? Is someone's spouse coming to one too many of our shows?"

"I'll cut to the chase. My brother, Rocket, is dead."

In the stunned silence that followed, I pulled out the calling card that had been signed with a kiss. Lexi's smile quavered, then fell entirely, as they reached for the card, examining first one side and then the other.

"I know he was collaborating with you on something. What I'd like to know is on what. What business were you and my brother involved in?"

There was a shift in the atmosphere, an almost imperceptible change, and I realized at that moment that I had asked exactly the wrong question. A look passed between merminx and octopus.

"Oh, detective, we couldn't possibly tell you that." Charisma said.

There was a long pause. When they didn't voluntarily elaborate, I asked—far calmer than I felt: "And why's that?"

I took the card back and pocketed it.

"Ms. Nightingale"—Lexi smiled apologetically—"Rocket was working with us in strictest confidence, and we are not at liberty to divulge information discussed under an NDA. I'm sure someone in your line of work can appreciate that, at least."

"So, what was it? Were you two and Rocket planning to open a second club or something? He was bankrolling you, is that it? Was his fiancé in on it?"

Lexi shook their head and long curls shimmered around their bare shoulders. Their every move was strategically designed to mesmerize. I blinked my gaze away, annoyed. "His business with us was our own," they said. "Disco never knew."

Or so they thought. Lexi sounded confident, but in my line of work I had learned to appreciate the uncanny sixth sense that long-term romantic partners tended to pick up about each other. I made a note to feel out just how little Disco actually knew about the Kraken Club next time I saw him.

"I'm sorry, Marrow. We both are." Lexi hit me with a remorseful, tear-shined pout from beneath a veil of thick silver lashes. "Rocket was a true blue sweetheart, and I hope you find who did him in. But we haven't spoken to Rocket in days. We had nothing to do with his death, and we have nothing more to say to you on the subject. Good luck, honey."

I stood up, jaw tense, and forced my face into a tight smile. It was clear that this was where I was supposed to smile in an understanding way, say good-night, and gracefully fuck off. The charm and sweet demeanor might have fooled their usual patrons, but the act was a harder sell on me.

"You've got a club to close up for the night, I understand," I said. "But you invited me back here I'm assuming for a reason."

"Yes, I recognized you from your picture in today's news," Lexi said. They tossed their hair impatiently. "Curiosity is a bad habit of mine, one I've been meaning to kick, and there's no time like the present. We are terribly sorry for your loss but you need to leave. Now."

"Did you put him up against Sealliance, is that it? Did these crates have something to do with your business arrangement? Can you say for *certain* that you two had nothing to do with his death?"

Lexi's eyes flicked to a space behind me and I felt a heavy hand landed on my shoulder. I turned to see the large bouncer from before looking down at me with calm unconcern.

"It's well past last call, detective." He squeezed a little, just enough to hint that I probably shouldn't try anything funny and gestured towards the door with his free hand. "Time you were on your way."

I wanted to punch someone even more, but I was no match for the doorman and when I looked back, Lexi and Charisma had already slipped away beneath the water.

"Yeah, yeah. I know the way out." I shrugged out of the goon's grip and left the club, aiming a two-fingered salute over my shoulders as I made my retreat.

Lexi was hiding something, no question. I was certain that they knew more about the circumstances surrounding Rocket's death. But what? And why?

I hadn't yet made it out of the Steam District when I got another buzz on my com. Figuring that it was likely Koko wondering where I'd gone, I pulled up the screen to fire off a hasty apology and instead found myself holding an invitation to the most exclusive of get-togethers from the woman who had so recently had me hauled off to Hab-Sec's central offices.

The message began with an animated crying emoji and read: *It was wrong of me to push you while you were mourning, darling. Bad form on my part. Blood sugar was low and that always makes me beastly. I'm having a last-minute clambake tonight and would love for you to join us. Allow me to make amends. XOXO, Campari.*

That didn't sound like the Campari Westwood that I knew. Then again, even the wealthiest and most well-connected among us carried superstitions about the dead. Perhaps the unwarranted accusation of fratricide had left the cold pall of bad luck hanging over her. Or maybe she wanted to throw a party just to lure me into causing an even bigger scandal for the next day's headlines. The more I thought on it, the likelier the latter sounded.

I left her message on read and put my com away without a response. When I got back to Koko's, he was already awake and getting ready for his day in the kitchen in a fur-lined gold paisley robe, flanked by a fresh pot of coffee and a thick stack of pancakes.

"Five more minutes and I was going to call HabSec and see if they'd hauled you in again," was all he said when I sat down at the kitchen table and poured a mug for each of us. He leaned in for a hug and raised one eyebrow as he caught wind of *eau de Kraken Club* on my jacket. "Your note said you were investigating a lead, yet you return to my home smelling of strip club. Did we have a good time?"

"I went to the Kraken to talk to Lexi Lagoon."

"The mermaid stripper?"

"That's the one. Met their octopus girlfriend, too. Quite the pair. Rocket was working with them on something, but when I mentioned him they clammed right up. None of this makes any sense, Koko."

"My money's on Campari." He sipped his coffee pensively. "You said Disco and Rocket were fighting because

Campari threatened to *expose* Disco for some unknown scandal and Rocket didn't back him up enough. What if Disco threatened to call off the wedding and Rocket mustered the courage to confront Campari?"

It was a stretch, but it was the most concrete motive I'd yet to suss out.

"Speaking of Campari, look what I just got." I pulled up Campari's message on my com and slid it across the table to Koko. I bit into and savored a mouthful of fluffy pancakes, butter, and syrup. The purest damned alchemy there is. Koko's eyebrows raised as he read and he gave a low whistle.

"A clambake at the *Westwood* estate. My, my, my. We're going to this, right?"

"You think I ought to?"

"I mean, it's obviously a trap. But so what if Campari's baiting you for a second lap around the news cycle? Attending this party is the *perfect* opportunity for you to snoop around her home! Maybe uncover the murder weapon; maybe find some pretty people to kiss away all our grief. Either way, we get to enjoy a top-notch soirée." He ate thoughtfully for a moment before adding: "Chances are high that the actual murderer will be there, right? I mean, even if Campari didn't do it, it's got to be someone Rocket knew. Someone we know. And if it's someone we know, they're going to be at this clambake."

I wasn't entirely sold on the idea, but it beat sitting at home and staring down the bottom of a bottle, waiting for the morgue or my parents to return my messages. Where were they, anyway?

"All right, I'll go. I take it you're my plus one?"

Koko's com chimed. He held it up to show off the invitation he'd just received. "Girl, you can be *my* plus one. Now finish your pancakes and try to get some rest before the hab lights come back on."

✳

At a certain income bracket, life in the habs is often lived one party to the next. Birthdays, holidays, engagements, weddings, casual mixers, afternoon cocktails, mid-week brunches: it doesn't matter how small or large the occasion, there's a type of party for it. A clambake is the most exclusive, secretive, anticipated party of all: a full-fledged bacchanalia in the sea.

I had seen the top story on *The Conch* that day: UNHINGED ADOPTED NIGHTINGALE SIBLING BRUTALLY ATTACKS BAR PATRONS: "I FEARED FOR MY LIFE," SAYS EDITOR-IN-CHIEF. So it was unsurprising when the butler who answered the door didn't believe me straight away when I said I had a personal invitation to the night's festivities. After scanning his tablet for a few moments, he pursed his lips and gestured for us to step into the pristine white tile foyer.

"The changing rooms are down the main corridor, on the left," he sniffed, still giving me stink-eye that could set off a noxious gas alarm. Koko and I blew him kisses as we pranced past him in bespoke ball gowns.

Campari's home unfolded around us into a temple dedicated to pop media. The lights were just barely bright enough to see our hands in front of us; every wall roiled and swerved around us, covered in projected scenes from long-lost movies from the eras before humanity fled the surface—when Hollywood still ruled supreme. Someone had mixed in clips of more modern stuff, like the one about the young man who leaves his hab with the help of his boyhood friend and a hooker with a heart of gold to find the True Meaning of Himself in the burnt-out surface settlements.

The projections in the parlor were static photographs of the original Electric Blue Moon, the yacht that had been sunk to ritually mark the founding of the habitat generations ago. A three-deck white pleasure craft in the middle of unbroken dark blue and nothing else. It seemed so small from the angle the photographer's drone had captured it. I could make out the vague, blurry shapes of people in short-sleeved shirts and bikinis. The thought of exposing one's skin to so much sun at once made my stomach crawl. Hard to imagine anyone not knowing about sun poisoning like that.

Koko tugged at my hand, drawing me away from the image and further into the house. Crystal chandeliers cast splintered fragments of pink light across a menagerie of furnishings and heirloom rugs, some in fabrics you could no longer manufacture. Guests sprawled, gathered, danced, prowled, and pawed amongst themselves in each room we passed. The library—lined floor to ceiling and wall to wall with real paper books! —had been rather cavalierly converted into the bar for the evening. A lithe, heavily tattooed boy stood behind a heavy table in a cloud of sandalwood-scented smoke and strained color-changing cocktails into coupe glasses.

Koko and I skipped those temptations and slipped through the thick maze of limbs and conversation towards our destination: the changing rooms at the end of the main hall. Because of course, everything up to that point was just the mood-setter. The true clambake was outside, beyond the safety features of the hab.

"Wish me luck out there, baby." Koko winked at me and I grinned back, momentarily taken outside of the recent tragic state of my life, swaddled in the hazy fantasia of wealth and excess.

"Happy hunting." A mad surge of laughter bubbled up from my chest as I stashed my coat, bag, and dress in a locker. In that moment it felt as though Rocket would surely be waiting for us on the other side of the airlock and all of the past few days would be revealed as a bad trip, nothing more.

Because I try to stay very on brand, the mersuit I slipped into was a glittering black number with a sleek dorsal fin edged in bioluminescent white. I settled my matching black breathing mask securely over my mouth and nose and connected it by way of a discrete tube down the nape of my neck to the black carcanet of artificial gills, styled to look like a sea serpent's skin, that hung at my bare shoulders and throat. That part was also lined with pale bioluminescent accents which pulsed gently with every breath I took.

Koko's was different in just about every other way, and far more expensive. His suit was made of all the colors of fire and passion that set off the cool, jewel undertones of his umber complexion to perfection. The design undulated like real flames thanks to the programmable fabric; to take it even further, he had added flaring side-fins to the tail and crowned himself with a gilded spiny crest that began at the brow of his smooth, shorn head and ended between the rippling muscles of his finely toned shoulder blades.

I gave Koko an enthusiastic thumbs-up, and he blew me an exaggerated kiss. Then I activated the exit, and together, we plunged into a bawdy dreamland of sound and light.

Remember the projected picture of *Electric Blue Moon* pre-sinking? The real deal lay dead and decaying right outside Campari's private airlock. It was a tradition, in the early days, when half of what was left of the population opted to set sail from the endless hellscape on land and never look back. At the opening ceremony for each hab, the founders would sink the yacht the hab was named after—usually the primary investor's favorite. We're told that it was a huge sacrifice at the time; a grand gesture to symbolize their true commitment and devotion to the new way of life. No going back once you sank your only way back to shore.

If you ask me, I think they couldn't figure out how to park a yacht in the middle of the ocean, and it was against whatever religion they held to to give away their now-useless toys to the sorry bastards they left stuck on the coast. Can't have the Poors sailing around in safe boats. Best just to sink them.

Koko and I paused to appreciate the presence of the wreck. The pile of charred beams, twisted metal, and broken windows lay on the bare ocean floor, barnacled and rusted. Perhaps when it first sank it had been a sight to see, but nearly a century underwater had turned it into an untended corpse. It looked more sad than inspirational. A burst of music rippled around us and we lost interest in the junked ship. We swam further into the sparkling heart of the clambake, waving to friends. Koko made eye contact with a pretty stranger and from there on out, I was on my own.

A cacophony of guests in haute couture mersuits danced to a jangly astralwave beat that thrummed through the water, broadcast directly into the sea through huge speakers. The DJ provided the beats from one of the delicate glass bubble rooms that had been temporarily tethered to the hab's outer hull. Each bubble had an air seal and an oxygen generator that allowed a handful of people to take off their masks and lounge on velvet couches to enjoy a drink, a snack, some designer drugs, and a lot of flirty banter.

It was a well-attended clambake, and the crème de la crème of society was out in full force. I recognized several people visiting from other habs. At a normal party, I would likely have been ostracized as a social pariah thanks to the day's headline news. The unspoken rule of a clambake, though, is to leave your real life at the front door. It lends an air of the unexpected and dangerous to the event; you never know if the person you're sharing a bubble with is an heiress or a murderer or both. What happens at each clambake is a set of stolen moments out of time; they are never spoken of again unless you want that clambake to be the last you're ever invited to.

As the hours rolled past, it was tempting to lose myself in the socializing and drugs, but I was there on a job and couldn't afford to get sidetracked. I kept moving from one group to the next, sharing laughs and drinks, never staying in one spot too long, always keeping my eyes and ears open.

As I swam towards a particularly popular bubble where a minor pop star was holding court around a buffet of spherified breakfast foods, I caught a flash of undulating red in the corner of my eye. Even amid the riot of colors, fantails, gilt breathing masks, and electro-animated makeup, Charisma stood out. No human could pull off tentacles that expressive.

And you bet your ass she wasn't alone. Lexi hovered close to her, beautiful but easy to mistake for any other partygoer in a mersuit, their back towards me. The two of them seemed tense, self-conscious almost. Which I suppose was understandable, given that they were—to my knowledge—the only two non-humans present.

I don't know much about octopus gesticulations, but I do know the telltale signs of a couple arguing in public and pretending not to. I swam over for a closer look. At clambakes, the music traveling through the water was always too loud to hear anyone through local com channels. If you weren't up in a bubble lounge, you used sign language to hold a conversation.

The near-constant parade of sparkling fins and pulsing holographic accessories passing between us made it hard for me to stay out of sight and still eavesdrop on their conversation. I caught Lexi signing "we need to go" and "foolish" and finally: "authorities . . . tracking."

After that, they were blocked from view by a group of partiers that parked themselves between us. I pushed around the dancers and got too close in my haste. Rookie mistake. Charisma's roaming eyes landed on me right away and widened in recognition. She tapped Lexi on the shoulder with one tentacle, and the two of them bolted without another word. *Damn.*

I pushed forward to chase after them when the entire ocean was plunged into sudden darkness and silence. Party guests were shadows ringed with bioluminescent paint, flitting in the dark like panicked wraiths. Looming above and beside us, Electric Blue Moon habitat was dead in the water. *Too* dead. I narrowed my eyes. Here and there, the dim orange glow of the backup emergency lights flickered to life, but there was something else. A more important element was missing: the air flow turbines weren't coming back on-line.

Power outages had been a near-daily annoyance for months, but they only ever lasted a few brief moments. As the seconds dragged on and the power stayed off, annoyed impatience grew into alarm, and confusion began to build from ripples into a full boil. I could hear several someones banging on the airlock doors. Panicked faces inside the hab pressed against the windows overlooking the yacht wreck.

"What the fuck is happening?" was a common refrain heard from several tinny com mics at once over the local channel.

A strange, alien movement tickled at my peripheral vision, and as I turned to look up at the massive dark silhouette of Electric Blue Moon, a cold shot of dread ran down my spine.

The longer I stared, the more I wondered if I were suffering the twin effects of too much grief and too little sleep. What else could I be facing down if not a hallucination? The diamond nanoweave outer hull of the hab, normally rigid and impenetrable, drooped. I watched as the walls slowly but surely slumping lower and lower like the heavy shoulders of an accountant at the end of a long and bloody tax season.

"Is anyone else seeing this crabshit?" I tried to swim through what had become a churning crowd of synthetic fins. A pulsing alarm wailed to life, loud and insistent. A staccato war drum beat of the desperate and helpless.

Someone tapped me on the shoulder and pressed something into my palm. I turned, thinking it must be Koko, but found only a dissipating cloud of bubbles in the murky orange half-light. Holding up a small, palm-sized clear cylinder, I thought someone had accidentally passed me drugs intended for someone else. Instead I found a rolled piece of paper rattling around inside the clear, airtight case.

Before I could hunt for my mystery note-passer, the hab power and life support systems whirred back on and the party garden was once more awash in festive lights and thumping beats. With a whoosh punctuated by a sturdy thump, the habitat walls straightened and solidified again. There were sighs of relief and cheers all around and then: a scream of pure terror. Shouts for help. A woman's voice cutting onto everyone's personal speaker feed seeking medical aid for someone outside.

It didn't take me long to find the source of distress. A crowd was gathering not far from where I swam. As I approached, I saw Campari Westwood's unmistakable bespoke mersuit floating limp in the water. I pushed through, heedless of those around me. It was Campari, face frozen in a rictus of pure horror, eyes wide and unblinking. Deader than Infinity's Cup on Global Detox Day.

I had to act fast before HabSec arrived. I pulled up my waterproof wrist com and snapped as many burst photos as I could before anyone could think to stop me. I managed to get in a few good shots before I was grabbed roughly from behind and dragged away from the body. Kitten, Campari's second-favorite section editor, shoved me into the airlock connected to the house, then spun me around to face his bulging, angry eyes and red-cheeked wrath.

"What the fuck are you doing here, Nightingale? Bit of a coincidence, you crashing Campari's party the same night someone sabotages both it and her suit? Now I find you taking photos of her like some kind of D-list tabloid ghoul? What is this: some kind of sick game to you?"

I scrambled to remove my breathing apparatus as Kitten hauled me up by my filtration collar.

"Easy!" I shrugged out of his grip and pulled myself onto a changing bench. "I had an invite! Campari herself—"

"—Did no such thing," he spat. "I personally oversaw that guest list, and you were definitely not on it."

"Seems like your boss had a change of heart and didn't bother to let you in on it," I shot back. "Maybe she didn't trust you anymore. Maybe you're the one that clocked her number just now. You seem awfully agitated, Kitten. What'd you do: conveniently forget to charge her suit's power pack?"

Outside, through the airlock window, I saw the red lights of a HabSec security sub flashing through the crowd. The door opened from the house side, and Varsity Beckett stepped into the room, flanked by half a dozen burly HabSec thugs.

"Chief! You're just in time to re-arrest Ms. Nightingale," Kitten scowled.

Varsity sighed and pinched the bridge of his nose. He hated being condescended to by rich kids almost as much as he hated my very existence. He looked as though he couldn't decide which of us to be most pissed at.

"I knew I shouldn't have let you out of my sight. Is *that* body outside your doing, Marrow?"

"Ugh, *no!*" Getting casually accused of murder multiple times in one week is even less fun than it sounds. "There's at least a dozen witnesses out there that can testify I wasn't with Campari when she died."

"There's still the matter of your trespassing at a *private* event," Kitten interjected. He turned back to Varsity. "How much are you going to let her get away with before you do your job and deport her, *officer*? How many more need to die before Marrow Nightingale is brought to justice?"

I realized Kitten was using his broadcast voice and looked down to see his com's recording light glowing. Varsity ignored the questions and addressed me instead.

"If we keep meeting like this, we're going to have to permanently reserve an interrogation room for you down at the station."

"This is pure bilge! I was an invited guest and I can prove it!"

Varsity waved me off impatiently, uninterested in viewing the invite on my com. He gestured for his HabSec goons to go out ahead of him to the crime scene before turning back to glare down at me. "Save it for your sworn statement, Nightingale. Now hurry up and get dressed or we'll carry you out in a fishing net as you are if we have to."

They left me to change out of my mersuit. The doorman had included my coat and bag with the rest of my things and I slipped the note capsule into my trench coat pocket. A sizeable crowd had formed by the time I emerged from the airlock. Cameras clicked and flashed from every angle as HabSec escorted me out of the mansion in yet another high-profile walk of shame. I thought I glimpsed

Koko's worried face in the back of the room, but it was hard to tell.

This was either going to tank my reputation as a detective or send demand for my services sky-high. Hard to say. Before we left the house, a familiar gold-dusted ivory shoulder jostled mine in the narrow hall and I swiveled to see Disco drunkenly stumble out of the bathroom, giggling. He turned and blinked at me with slow surprise.

"Disco?" I asked. "Disco what are you doing here? Hey! Have you heard from my parents yet? Can you come with me to the station?"

"Oh, hey, sis," he slurred. "Great party, right?"

Then he laughed, and it came out thin, too high, borderline hysterical. I'd never heard him like that before. Too stunned to reply, I let the officers half-drag me through the furiously live-vlogging crowd while I craned my neck to watch Disco disappear into the depths of Campari's mansion.

I found myself once again at HabSec's central office; this time I sat in a swathe of black tulle and ten inch heels, my hands cuffed in front of me to a cold metal table in a maddeningly beige room. I'd already given my full statement to a staff officer and been subjected to a bot-administered lie detector test and cross-examination.

Just as I thought about alleviating my boredom through wordless screaming, Varsity pushed briskly through the door and straddled the chair across from me. He tossed a data tablet on the table and glared expectantly at me. Overhead, stark, cold lights flickered intermittently.

"What's the deal with the power lately?" I asked him conversationally. "Someone forget to pay the bills?"

Varsity ignored the question. He took a long pull from a vape and exhaled out the side of his mouth. He stared at me like I was an incomplete table puzzle and he was trying to figure out which piece had gone missing.

"Marrow, level with me. How many more times are we going to do this in the next, say, forty-eight hours? Two? Three? Are you stalking people now? You've always been a pain in my ass, but you've never been what I'd call unhinged."

I sighed, exhausted.

"Varsity, I'm telling you, I had a legitimate invitation to be at that party. Campari sent me a message this morning, something about wanting to make amends and clear the air. You and I disagree on a lot, but when have you ever known me to crash a party? That's just bad for business. I have a reputation among my clientele to uphold." He kept staring until I wanted to bang my face on the table just to have something more interesting to do than try to reason with him. "The doorman checked a list before admitting me! It was a clambake, for fuck's sake! You don't even know the time and place unless you're invited."

"Well, I wouldn't know anything about that." He wouldn't, and it probably ate him up inside that he would never get called out to one unless a body turned up. "And you just happened to be around when the woman you attacked in a bar fight goes full goldfish?"

I didn't have time for this. I had proof of invitation and no weapon on me, not to mention both myself and Campari had been surrounded by witnesses that could attest to my innocence. Varsity didn't have anything on me, and he knew it.

"It's late and I've given you my statement. So if you have no further questions, *officer*, I really have to get back to work."

"Let me see it."

"See what?"

"The fucking invite to the fucking party!"

I rolled my eyes and flicked the message file, forwarding it over from my com to his. As he reviewed it, I kept my eyes focused pointedly on the door. Varsity eventually let out a long-suffering sigh, looked up at me, and came around the table to unlock my cuffs.

"Alright, Nightingale, you're free to go for now. But this is a lot of heat and a lot of publicity. Kitten's got your face on every gossip channel and half the legit news channels. A lot of people want to see you topside and I happen to be one of them.. If you value your lifestyle here in the hab—in any hab, really—do yourself a favor and quit showing up at murder scenes. Let me do my job, and stay out of my way. Maybe you should think about joining your parents out on Fashima's Escape."

How the fuck did Varsity know where my parents were? And what were they doing on Fashima's Escape? It was a secluded, if second-rate, casino hab popular with honeymooners and gambling competitions. Not the sort of place my parents would usually frequent.

"Trying to get rid of me one way or another, huh?" I slipped in to my snakeskin trench coat and grabbed my satchel. "Officer Beckett, before I go. Do you have anything on my brother's case yet?"

"You mean besides the fact that someone put a bullet in his head?" He stared sullenly at me, but I caught a glint of thoughtful curiosity in his eyes. "You've really got nothing this time, do you? Well, well, well."

"Come on, man."

Varsity collected his tablet off the interrogation room table and joined me at the door. He looked into my eyes for just a moment, then looked away, rubbing at his chin.

"I'm afraid I can't divulge the details of an ongoing investigation. Especially not with a person of interest in the case. Take care, Marrow. Do have a safe trip home."

What an asshole. With no one else willing to talk, the

morgue was my only hope for getting some goddamned answers and they were still radio silent. I shoved my hands into the pockets of my coat and felt a cool, smooth glass cylinder brush against my left knuckles. I'd been held up at HabSec for so long, I'd nearly forgotten about the mystery note slipped to me at the clambake when the lights went off.

I ducked around the corner of a building into a service alley and opened the cylinder, unscrolling the paper inside. It displayed a download glyph that I could scan with my com. Beneath that, a message was printed in all caps: *TALKED TO MUSTANG XASHA'S BABY LATELY?*

Mustang Xasha, the wealthy son and heir of Ta$ia and Calliope Xasha, the genius power couple who had founded Sealliance Corp? What did that little rich fuck have to do with anything? And since when did he have a kid? I ignored the glyph for the time being—it was likely malware anyway. I needed to settle in somewhere familiar and relatively secure and do the one thing I was actually pretty good at: deep research.

I stopped by my place to pick up my gear and a change of clothes, plus a couple of pain killers to come along for the ride. I tried to clean up from the clambake, but only succeeded in smudging my eyeliner into a glittery mess of black kohl and holographic blue mica. I kept my hair in a black shaggy long pixie which didn't need a lot of maintenance under normal circumstances, but even that had fallen victim to too many nights without a proper shampoo. I tousled in a few shakes of dry shampoo and resigned myself to looking like a walking disaster. Wouldn't be the first time I'd holed up at Infinity's in such a state.

I was so out of it that I didn't realize it was already nine the next morning. Varsity had kept me at the station far longer than I had thought. The bigger surprise for me was that Infinity's was actually open at such an hour, and for brunch, no less. Disoriented, I pushed through the doors and found myself surrounded by a wholly alien subset of the population: the desk jockeys and ad agents of Electric Blue Moon, all out for their loud mid-morning power breakfasts. The normally dim lights were far too bright. The live DJ had been swapped out for a peppy lo-fi pre-recorded mix. I had to wonder if I was breaking any records for how quickly I was jumping from one nightmare to the next these days.

Undaunted, I moved unsteadily towards my usual table only to be swiftly intercepted by a pretty young woman wielding a digital menu. Her nametag read "Liberty Bravo." Since when did Infinity's staff wear name tags?

"Welcome to Infinity's Cup," Liberty beamed at me.

"Uh, hi." I tried to brush past her with a weak smile and a gesture towards my table, but she thwarted my maneuver.

"Do you have a reservation for brunch?"

"Please, I'm not usually here before five. I just need a Sharkbite and some alone time," I begged.

Liberty looked me over with an assessing eye and took in the bags beneath my eyes, the way my hair refused to lay flat, the hungover hunch of my shoulders, and relented.

"Would you like a seat at the bar?"

I shook my head and continued towards the leatherette sanctuary of my booth. "This table's fine." I knew I was pushing it and being a bit of an asshole besides, but it seemed Liberty had decided to take pity on me.

"One Sharkbite coming up."

She left, and as I settled in to the familiar squeaky cushioned bench, it occurred to me to take out my com to check the feeds and catch up on life. There were plenty of pics from last night's already infamous clambake, but I couldn't find any that featured Lexi or Charisma. You'd think an actual mermaid accompanied by a talking octopus would have been a bigger deal. Evidently I'd stolen the show.

Post after post of my angry mug being "escorted" out of Campari's posh home scrolled past my eyes. This was going to be difficult to recover from, career-wise, but I didn't have time to dwell. Somewhere in there was a shot of the murderer. There had to be. I looked for time-stamps, trying to find the last pictures taken of Campari before the hab had gone dark.

The last picture I could find of Campari alive, she was lounging in a bubble with an arm draped around Disco's shoulders. One of Campari's writers sat close to them, caught in the open-mouthed act of telling a story. The photo was taken at half-past midnight. After that, nothing.

I moved on to my own photos, taken at a quarter past two, zooming in on various details of the body as much as the com would allow. The server came by to drop off my drink, which I sipped gratefully as I stared at Campari's dead-eyed gaze, willing it to become something useful. Something coherent.

Frustrated, I pulled up a browser and searched for news on Mustang Xasha. There were the usual piles of PR bullshit to wade through: trumped up anecdotes about Xasha's boundless philanthropy, environmental fact-finding missions to the surface, and, of course, his genius with advanced synthetic intelligence.

I unrolled the note again, and this time I scanned the glyph. I braced myself for my com to succumb to whatever nefarious programming I was about to download. I entertained the brief thought that it might spontaneously combust and wondered how many ad-executives I could hit with it on my way out.

Instead, my screen brightened with a grainy, low-budget video—some kind of documentary from Sealliance's robotics department. Mustang was in the process of tak-

ing apart a biosynthetic robot skull to show off the in-
sides. I half-watched it on mute as I nursed my drink,
and damn near almost missed the part where he showed
the robot's face. I went back in the video and paused at
the reveal. There he was, lifeless and empty-eyed but unmistakable: Disco Bishop. Or at least, Disco's face, peeled
back to expose ceramic disks and fine machinery.

My mind reeled. I tried to steady it with a big gulp of
spicy tomato juice and salty kelp vodka. Coincidence.
Had to be. Or maybe Disco had seen one of Sealliance's
bots somewhere, took a fancy to the aesthetic, and had
reconstructive surgery done to look like one of them.
People did weird shit like that, from time to time. Hell.

I cracked a piece of ice between my teeth and tried out
another thought: Disco was a good-looking guy and a
well-known fashion model. Maybe he'd sold his likeness
to Sealliance to use on their bots. A perfectly reasonable
explanation for why I was watching Mustang Xasha put
my brother's fiancé together like a kid's toy assembly kit.

In spite of my strong desire to cling to reason, I looked
up the documentary's film date. 2101. Eleven years ago,
which would have made Disco somewhere around thir-
teen years old, far too young for that face. I choked down
a curse with another gulp of my drink and pulled up a
recent picture of Disco on my screen. Then, wincing at
the prohibitive cost of the transaction, I connected to SeaNet—the global version of HabNet—and I purchased a
facial recognition image search.

SeaNet was slow and glitchy, even when paying a pre-
mium—another casualty of the information wars. I had
time to savor my Sharkbite and order another while Sea-
Net labored to haul up my search results.

The more recent matches were what I had expected
to find: glamorous shots of Disco by himself, Disco in
fashion spreads, Disco making guest appearances, Disco

and friends at parties, Disco and Rocket. I paused on a shot of them taken only a couple weeks back at a museum gala. They were luminous, mythic almost, in the way they both wore glamour like a second skin. The way the two of them looked as though they were born to be the center of everyone's attention. Rocket looked genuinely happy.

I lingered on his smile for a moment, then paid extra to download that picture to my personal drive. I kept scrolling, and the more I dug, the wonkier the search results got. At first, I thought perhaps the algorithm was wrong. Sure, there were a few legitimate mismatches in Disco's search results, but then I found a recurring theme. Photos from three years back on a different hab, all with the same wrong name: *Winter Mason*. It was Disco in those pictures, but the captions described him as someone's garment-boy—a combination house-cleaner and personal assistant popular among the trendy set. In each one, they referred to him by the name "Winter Mason."

I kept scrolling. It was always possible the pictures had been batch mislabeled. Or maybe Winter had been Disco's garment-boy at some point. As more images of Disco turned up with Winter Mason's name, another thought occurred to me: when had Disco moved to Electric Blue Moon? Two years ago? Maybe this is who Disco was before he landed his first modeling gig. It wasn't wholly unheard of for a working-class immigrant from the surface to get a lucky break and reinvent themselves into something more palatable to the rich.

I ran a news and location search for Winter Mason, expecting the network to back up my theory and help me down from the shaky ladder of wild conspiracy theories I'd found myself stuck on. Instead, it knocked a few more rungs out from under my feet, leaving me dangling.

Winter Mason's time in the news reels was cut short two and a half years ago. He was listed on the rolls as one of the eighty thousand lives lost when the Krill Intentions habitat had experienced a devastating power failure and collapsed, killing nearly everyone inside.

First, he was a robot prototype; then, a garment boy killed in a mass tragedy; now, a supermodel engaged to the most influential young billionaire in Electric Blue Moon. It added up to something big, but I'd be damned if I could see the full picture from where I sat.

"Get you anything else, hon?" Liberty asked, interrupting my musing.

"No time." I got up and settled my bill, tossing on a generous tip along with my default five-star rating. I doubted that Infinity cared for that sort of bullshit, but Liberty would need those stars on her record if she ever wanted to vie for a different service contract. "See you around, kid."

I had to get into the morgue and see Rocket's body for myself, and fast—if it wasn't too late already. It couldn't be a coincidence that his corpse had been neatly swept away before any of his family or the local authorities could get a look at him, and that the last person to see his body at all was evidently a ghost himself. If the footage I was looking at was real, had Rocket known? Had he confronted his fiancé?

My com buzzed and Disco's name glowed on the display. How did that old saying go? *Speak of the devil?*

"Disco, baby, hell of a party last night, right? I didn't expect to hear from you so soon. What's your status?"

"Marrow! Can you even believe it? Two murders in one week! I'm going to need a serious deep soul cleanse this weekend. Like an extra-long hot quartz bath, you know? I've never seen so much death in all my life!"

Eighty thousand dead said otherwise.

"Yeah, real gonzo stuff, kid. Where are you now?"

He ignored my question and kept talking.

"Listen, Mare, the clambake going awry put an idea into my head. We haven't given Rocket a real farewell yet, you know? And so I thought, why not pull together a last-minute affair tonight? Well, not technically tonight—four A. M. tomorrow, so we can start in the dark and hold vigil until the morning lights come on. I'm calling it a *mourning party*. To say good-bye to Rocky. Clever, right?"

"Do you mean a wake?"

"Yeah, that's the thing. But mine's got a better name. So you'll come, right? You'll be there? I know it's super late notice, but it would mean so much. Rocket would have wanted you there."

"Wouldn't miss it for the world, babe. See you then."

I ended the transmission and half-jogged the rest of the way to the morgue. Disco would have known about Gucci's wake and would never have settled for doing the same thing in such short order, under normal circumstances. The Disco I knew would have waited until the funeral and turned it into a massive gala. I had only a few hours to figure out what had happened to Rocket—and to divine what Disco had planned next.

Access to Electric Blue Moon's morgue, like all sensitive sections, is heavily policed in segmented checkpoints. The head-down-talking-furiously-on-the-phone routine while I tagged along with a group of lab techs got me past the front desk and through the lobby just fine. An access card I'd won in a card game a couple months back got me past the first employee entrance and down a flight of clammy metal stairs. An old-fashioned set of lockpicks got me through the next rusting set of double doors, and then I stood at one end of a long, cold, fluorescent-bleached hallway.

The first three doors were filing rooms and offices, each unlocked and thankfully unoccupied. Midway down the hall, I found the one I needed: wide double-doors big enough for gurneys and a crisp sign above that read: COLD STORAGE. My satisfied smile lasted only long enough for me to push through the doors and run straight into an apron-garbed orderly.

"Who the fuck are you?" She frowned, scrambling to pull her hair out of her eyes. I squinted a little and assessed. She was on the young side, trendy makeup and hair. A backpack slumped against the nearby intake desk, and a student's tablet on said desk was opened to a Hab-Net social profile.

"You the new intern?" I asked dismissively, shifting my posture and body-language to signal *busier and more important than you*. I scanned her up and down with a swift flick of my eyelashes and saw her shoulders slump almost imperceptibly.

"I mean I've been here for three weeks now," she replied with an edge of defensiveness. "My name is Palisade."

"Yeah, great, welcome to the team. Look, you've met Mall, right?"

She bit her lip and tried to keep her eyes from widening in front of me—a surly, imperious stranger. "Yeah . . ." she said warily.

It was an easy guess. Pretty much every office has someone working middle management named Mall Something-or-Other. It was the sort of common name that always managed to make it only so far up the corporate ladders. If the intern had mustered the presence of mind to ask me for a last name, I'd have been in trouble.

"Great, well, I'm working a case with him," I flashed my very official-looking private detective's license long enough for the gold foil to look properly shiny. "I had an appointment today to see a body."

Palisade frowned again. "He didn't mention anything about an appointment. What was your name, again?"

I rolled my eyes and pulled up my com. "Listen, sorry if he doesn't update your internal calendar or whatever, but I'm really on a deadline here. Can you just, I don't know, go ahead and open the drawer? I promise I'm not here to touch anything, I just need to confirm a few facts. For the case." When she hesitated I added, "Mall's standard fee is fifty doubloons but, since he's not here to accept it . . ."

I let the implication of easy money float between us until she grasped what I was getting at. Her eyes widened again.

"Uh, yeah. Of course." She sat down at the desk and pulled up the lock chart to the corpse drawers. "Which one was it?"

"Nightingale. Rocket Nightingale." I sent the money to her personal com and she pocketed it with an offhand flick of her finger.

"Oh wow, *high* profile," she said, tapping in the unlock code. "HabSec keeps calling us about that one."

A latch clicked open on the wall and a drawer popped out just an inch. "Oh yeah? You ever field any of those calls?"

Palisade shook her head. "Mall does, usually, or some other on-shift supervisor. Mostly it's just us telling them to go fuck each other."

"Yeah, that's probably the best answer to give them."

I stood in front of the waiting drawer. A digital readout panel just above the cold, steel handle scrolled his name over and over in green and black: NIGHTINGALE, ROCKET #596-32-09112112.

I blinked once, twice, took a deep breath of clinical, cold air through my nose and then released it through clenched teeth. I could feel the intern staring at my back, wondering when the fuck I was going to get on with whatever it was I'd paid her fifty doubloons for. I closed my fingers around the handle and yanked it open abruptly, staggering back as the unexpectedly light drawer came rattling out.

"Well, that's weird."

The intern peered over my shoulder at the empty drawer. Empty. HabSec and I were being given the run-around by the morgue not because of red tape, but because there was no body in the first place. Ice ran through my veins. I spun around and grabbed the intern's shoulders.

"The body. Where is it? Where would anyone take him—it?"

"I don't—I don't know! He was processed fast; I barely got a look at the toe tag."

"The autopsy room, maybe?" I asked, hoping against hope.

She shook her head. "It was marked as concluded!"

Footsteps echoed in the hall outside. I was out of time, but there was no way I was leaving that place empty-handed. There was another door at the back of the cold room; I gestured to it with my chin. "Where's that go?"

"The coroner's office." She blinked back her nervousness and lifted her head boldly. "Do you really have an appointment to meet with Mall today?"

Hell, might as well give the kid a real on-the-job education. I relaxed my grip on her shoulders and nudged a smile at the corners of my mouth.

"Sure I do. How about five hundred doubloons says you're Mall for the day?"

The footsteps outside drew closer, accompanied by a tuneless whistle. Palisade looked back at me and nodded.

"Six hundred."

On a normal case I would have balked at the blatant shakedown, but I had to make a one-time exception in the moment. For myself as much as Rocket. I tapped the bribe over with only a fleeting scowl. "Don't get used to this kind of payout. Nice to see you again, Mall."

I locked the door behind me for good measure and took stock. It was a quiet, small, dark office with not much in the way of a personality. A couple of holophotos from past vacations on the wall, a tasteful painting of some undersea ruins, copies of the coroner's diplomas—of course. A few potted plants. An engraved wood-paneled vape pen. A couch against one wall, the kind you can pull out into an uncomfortable bed.

And there, blinking softly in its docking station on the desk: the coroner's work tablet. I heard the main door to the cold room open and a deeper voice speaking to the intern, both of them too muffled to make out. If she decided to rat me out, there wouldn't be a lot I could do about it, so I hoped six hundred doubloons was enough to buy a few minutes of silence. I turned my attention back to the tablet and plugged a password cracker into the input port. In a matter of moments, Rocket's file was up. I started the download process to transfer the file to my com and read while I waited.

> *Security Class Black: Government Client Confidential.*
> *Subject: Rocket Nightingale.*
> *Property of Palaimon Life Systems Incorporated.*
> *Subject sustained heavy damage from a single bullet administered directly to the skull's internal black box. Short term memory log damaged beyond repair and file is irretrievable. Subject has been transferred to a rehabilitation facility for overall repair and therapy. Send all further updates to Kline Nightingale.*

A lot of those words sounded an awful lot like the terms thrown around in the Sealliance documentary I'd just watched. The back of my neck itched uncomfortably.

I scrolled through Rocket's file and found photographs of his body, the wound, and then almost impossibly, Rocket's head splayed apart to reveal a network of wires and lights. Broken and splintered, but otherwise practically identical to the inner workings of the Disco look-alike I'd watched in the earlier video.

The download finished, and I hastily backed out of the file and put the tablet back on the desk. I didn't know what the hell was going on, but I knew I needed to get out of the morgue with that information intact.

I waited until I heard the main door to the cold room open and shut, then waited a few minutes more just to sure. Cautiously, I opened the door a crack and peeked into the adjoining room. Palisade gave me an all-clear sign before returning to her social network feed. I nodded, closed up the coroner's office behind me, then made my way back up to the main lobby. My gut told me I'd just used up all the good luck I was going to have on this case in one go.

Back on the streets, still reeling from what I had discovered, I considered my options. Disco's party was half a day away; I had already been to Infinity's once that day and didn't want him to start charging me rent for that booth. My place was still swarming with paparazzi—if anything, there were three times as many now than there had been just a day earlier—and I didn't want to impose on Koko's hospitality yet again.

Times like these, I'd normally go over to Rocket's office for a few hours and annoy him while he tried to get work done. But now Rocket was dead—not just dead, a dead robot. His fiancé was either a live robot or a ghost or some third option I hadn't even conceived of yet. Nothing made a damned bit of sense. I was unmoored, adrift in a surreal sea of death and secret robot identities. Maybe that was why I eventually found myself walking into the Steam District and through the doors of the Kraken Club.

❋

Lexi wasn't performing, but there were three human dancers in mersuits putting on a solid show. I made straight for the bar and ordered a seaweed gin, neat.

"Leave the bottle," I said, just to have a reason to sit there indefinitely. The bar-bot on duty made a note of how full the bottle was and rolled away to do robot things elsewhere.

After a shot, my hands shook less. I pulled up the file and began to read it again from the top. Rocket—the brother I had grown up with almost my whole life—was an android? When exactly had that happened? Had he been one the whole time, or was he swapped at some point? There was no mention in the file, as though whomever it was intended for would have known this information as a matter of course. It was all like something out of an old teledrama.

Okay, so a secret android brother, two high-profile deaths. A whole lot of cover-up. And a fashion model with a secret past as a garment-boy who may also be an android. Not that the garment-boy part mattered that much. I would have been in the same line of work, had my adopted rich parents not gotten my biological *poor* parents killed.

The Nightingales. A memory blared sirens through my shell-shocked mind and I scrolled back up to the top of Rocket's file. *Palaimon Life Systems.* I'd heard that name before.

For most of my adult life, I'd made a point of ignoring the bulk of my family's businesses. There was always some suspicious executive watching, waiting for me to seize control of the executive office with a parrot on my shoulder or whatever the hell it was they thought poor orphans did when we didn't remember our place in the natural order of things. So I showed them by becoming allergic to the boardroom. But I still had to hear all about it at family dinners.

Palaimon Life Systems was one of my mom's companies. Small, but hungry, like Mom always seemed to be. I vaguely recalled last year, her frustration at the Electric Blue Moon board of directors for not granting her company the life support systems contract for the hab when Sealliance's ten-year contract had come up for renewal. In spite of her best efforts, they chose to stick with the devil they knew, like nearly every other hab in the seas.

"Cheaper, faster, more localized resources just make sense!" She moaned over dinner. *"What are these imbeciles so afraid of from Sealliance? That kraken can afford to lose one hab contract."*

And now she and Dad were conspicuously absent from the hab, and her life systems corp's name was stamped into her son's synthetic flesh.

A flash of tentacles caught my attention from the back hall, just barely visible from my vantage point at the bar. If there was a chance I could get Charisma to open up about what she and Lexi had been doing at Campari's clambake, I needed to take it.

I left the bar and followed quickly, just in time to see her disappear through a door marked as an emergency hab airlock exit. *Damn.* I'd need a suit to follow, and even then it wouldn't be subtle. I glanced both ways down the hall and saw no trace of anyone else. With no way to follow Charisma further and no security in sight, I settled on second best: brazenly snooping through their dressing quarters.

I loitered in the hall long enough to be certain that Charisma wasn't going to pop back in, then picked the lock to the dressing room and let myself in. The Sealliance crates were still secured with the biolocks that would only open for the intended recipient. A roadblock for some, perhaps. Not this Nightingale.

I borrowed one of Lexi's hairbrushes from her dressing table and carefully lifted a few stray hairs caught in the tines. I took the protective case off my com and carefully peeled out a delicate, glossy transfer sheet from the inner lining. I set the hairs on the sheet and then folded it first lengthwise and then widthwise. Then I stuck the thing in my mouth and let the heat and organic materials work their magic. In the process, I discovered it was mint-flavored.

After thirty seconds, I carefully extracted the packet, unfolded it, and wiped it over the top biolock like a moist towelette. A friendly green light came on at the same time as the crate clicked open. Just goes to show, sometimes you really *can* find a great deal at a late-night swap meet.

Inside the top crate were all the makings of a top-notch surgical ward: hand tools, PPP supplies, semi-autonomous robotic packages, tiny sanitation bots, and several mysterious devices that I couldn't begin to name. Our hab medical units would have passed out from joy at receiving the tech Lexi had lying around their dressing room.

Even more interesting, much of it was modified. When I picked up a scalpel, for instance, it didn't quite fit right in my hand. Wrapped up in an octopus's tentacle, however, I suspected it would fit perfectly. Was Charisma still working as a surgeon on the side? Surgical equipment in the back room of a strip club wasn't in itself anything damning. For all I knew I had stumbled upon an unlicensed butt implant operation. But this was Sealliance contraband and locked with the highest security. I needed to know what the two of them had brought into Electric Blue Moon with them. I moved to the console affixed to the wall just above the surface of Lexi's lounge pool to see if I could uncover answers.

The computer was running high-security corporate encryption, too powerful for my normal cracker. But my career as a P.I. would have been short-lived if I hadn't innovated ways to dig in to wealthy people's secrets. I slipped a gold snake bangle off my wrist and unscrewed the serpent's head to reveal the hidden cracking chip inside.

The bangle was a bespoke accessory designed for me by one of the best fashion houses in the business, and it had cost me the entirety of my tuition allowance for university. The Nightingales had been furious, of course, but in a way I think it helped. When they found out I had spent a sizable amount of money on a bracelet, I became just like all the other rich kids. They treated me a little more like family after that. Once they'd finished screaming at me for throwing my future away on fashion trends. What they didn't know was what I kept inside it, of course. I took a moment to admire the serpent's red jeweled eyes glinting in the light before setting to work on the console.

"Well I'll be damned and drowned," I breathed. As I combed through Lexi's files, it quickly became evident that this was absolutely not a butt implant operation.

I was so focused on the wealth of diagrams and receipts glowing on the screen that I almost didn't catch the sound of heavy footsteps hurrying down the hall in my direction. I slipped my bracelet back around my wrist, turned off the console monitor, and then hastily unplugged the console to cover up my digging. By the time the large bouncer rushed into the room, stun gun drawn, I was sitting innocently on the cushioned bench, earbuds in my ears, playing a dumb jewel-collecting game on my com.

"What the fuck do you think you're doing back here?" He loomed over me. I glanced up with a look of embarrassed surprise and took my earbuds out.

"Easy, pal." I held up my hands and gave him a flirty smile. "I just had a few follow-up questions for Lexi. I figured they wouldn't mind if I made myself at home."

"Well you figured wrong, *pal*. Lexi ain't here right now and this is a private space. You've got three seconds to get out of here on your own two legs before I throw you out."

I wasn't about to argue with the huge man with a stun gun. I shrugged and squeezed past him into the hall and left to go catch a nap. I would need to be at my best to make it through Disco's mourning party that night.

After a luxuriant six hours of sleep, I fixed myself a breakfast shake and drank it in the bathtub while I finally washed off the last few days from my criminally parched skin. I mulled over what I'd learned on Lexi's console. At first glance, it looked like blueprints for advanced mersuits. For their dancers, maybe. But then their schematics went deeper—neuro networks, synthetic nervous systems, regenerative tissues spliced from half a dozen organisms. They weren't just building mersuits, they were combining Sealliance's android technology with the genetics that made Lexi possible. They were aiming to transfer living consciousness into brand new merbodies.

Snake oil—that's what Lexi and Charisma were selling. It had to be. I hoped for their sakes that's all it was because if not, those two were in way over their heads. And they would take all of Electric Blue Moon down with them sooner or later. It was only a matter of time before Sealliance struck again.

Which brought me to the other mystery at hand: Disco Bishop, aka Winter Mason. Ghost? Robot? Robot ghost? What was his connection to all of this? Was Disco another hunted corporate refugee like Lexi, or was he Mustang Xasha's pet crack saboteur?

As if to underscore my thoughts, the power flickered and died. Outside my bathroom window was nothing but suffocating dark. Someone in the distance shouted angrily, their frustration echoing off the buildings.

A memory teased the edge of my mind. Something about Krill Intentions' research lab. They had been on the news days before their system failure. Their research team had been on the brink of a big breakthrough in nanoweave regeneration technology. There had been moves to take their entire habitat off the Sealliance grid and go fully independent. My mother had been thrilled about it—proof she could take to Electric Blue Moon's board that independence was possible.

Krill Intentions had tried to break free from Sealliance, and their hab had been destroyed. Now my mother was devoting most of her corporate resources to pushing Electric Blue Moon towards the same independence, and our hab was harboring valuable Sealliance tech that threatened to propagate itself throughout the seas. Were our intermittent outages warning shots?

The power flickered back to life, breaking me from my thoughts. I climbed out of the bath, toweled off, and changed into a slinky black evening gown that streamed glowing gothic poetry along the skirt. *"Our cups are polished skulls 'round which the roses twine..."*

In the mirror, tired brown eyes stared back at me through smoky eye makeup. My pale complexion had been made paler by fatigue and poor nutrition choices. "Just get this job done, kid," I told myself. "Just see this through, for Rocket, and we'll say to Hell with all of them after that. That's a fucking promise."

At least I had an excuse to wear this dress.

The man of the hour greeted me himself at the door. He was draped in a romantically flowing, seaglass green taffeta poet's shirt that cut a deep vee down to his chiseled and waxed abs. He threw his super-model arms around me in a welcome hug and squealed with delight, as though my arrival was an utter surprise.

"I'm so glad you could make it!" He squeezed me tight, like we hadn't seen each other in months. I was eerily reminded of another hug from him in this same foyer a few days ago.

I forced myself to speak, tried not to search for the machine behind the skin and teeth. "How ya been holding up, kid?"

"Getting by one day at a time." A tremor of emotion ran through his words, but it seemed there was a hardness in the back of his gaze as he pulled away. Had I looked a little too long? Did he know that I knew?

In a blink the coldness melted into a watery smile and I was left only with speculation. Disco took my arm in his and escorted me to the lounge where a dozen mutual friends were in attendance. I waved to Koko, who was holding court near the fireplace, and he blew me a kiss without missing a beat of his conversation.

"You're going to adore the menu," Disco told me. "Along with a very *special* little appetizer—wink, wink—Chef is preparing chilled garden soup, soya fritters, and a *literal rainbow* of sushi."

The pure nausea must have been written all over my face. Everyone has a texture that sets their stomach on edge and runs rusty nails over the chalkboard of their spine. Mine happened to be raw fish.

"Fuck, that's right! You *hate* sushi! I'm such an idiot. Marrow, I'm so sorry honestly. With everything going on, I'd completely forgotten, and when Chef showed me his proposal for tonight's main course I was so utterly enchanted—oh, say you don't absolutely loathe me, please!"

"Of course I don't." How could I hate someone I didn't really know?

"I'm so glad! I mean, you're still like a sister to me, right? No matter what the future holds. Kindred spirits, that's what we are. I felt it from the first moment we met. I think I'll probably *always* call you my sister. Anyway, here." He set a glass of champagne in my hand. "After dinner we'll all swim outside and give Rocket a clambake send-off like no one's ever *seen* before. When the feeds get our footage, your little spat with Campari will be ancient history!"

The kitchen bell chimed and Disco excused himself before I could remind him that Campari was dead, too. I sipped my champagne moodily and glared down any of the other guests who looked like they were looking for small talk.

When Disco returned, he led a parade of impeccably groomed waitstaff bearing trays of fine cuisine. All of us in the lounge set aside our drinks and followed obediently into the dining room with more than a little anticipation.

It was assigned seating; our names glowed up at us from digital markers affixed to the napkins, and at each place setting, a small jewel-encrusted scalloped clamshell waited for us. As we took our seats and opened them, we discovered each of us had been gifted with a glittering square pink pill.

Guests exchanged knowing smiles and surreptitious, excited whispers. Next to me, Koko covered his mouth with his hands in delighted surprise.

"Have you ever had this before, baby?" he asked as he lifted his pill into the light on the tip of a dainty pinky finger. "It's a limited-edition mind-candy made by a truly lush alchemist out on Smells Like Sea Spirit habitat. It's called Tiny Dancer, and it will have your brain doing velvet pirouettes *all* night long."

He popped his tablet gleefully between his teeth and washed it down with champagne. "Disco's more well-connected than I thought. Even I couldn't score a dinner party's worth of Tiny Dancer."

If that intel is right, Disco is the most well-connected person on the planet, I thought. I closed the lid on my own clamshell with no small amount of regret and set it aside. I had no idea how my system might react to a new drug, but I hoped I'd be able to find out later, once the job was done. For the time, it was best that I stuck to the bubbles and crème de cassis.

Dome-covered plates were carefully set in front of us soon after. At the head of the table, Disco raised his glass in my direction with a smile and a wink.

"Had Chef make you something special, mama."

The server whisked away my dome to reveal plump, fragrant steamed soup dumplings, a particular favorite of mine. The rich scent of mushrooms and herbs blooming out from the delicate red parcels set my mouth watering. Disco stood up and raised his glass, bringing the table's attention to him. We all quieted down and prepared for a speech.

"All right, everyone. We all know how these things usually go. Bla bla, rehearsed monologues and so forth while the drugs kick in and our food gets cold!" Knowing laughter tittered around us. "But I'm sure we also remember how Rocket was never a fan of a wait, and tonight is in his honor, after all. So speeches and stories will come soon enough. For now, to Rocket."

"To Rocket," we echoed, and clinked glasses with our neighbors.

Everyone around me began to eat heartily, some already reaching for second and third glasses of the good wine close at hand. I looked at my plate through narrowed eyes. Disco knew I hated sushi and loved dumplings. And he also knew I was actively investigating the death of his fiancé. On the other hand, he was the one who had insisted I take the case to begin with. Why hire me to do a job just to murder me in the process? I stared at my dumplings and wondered if there was such a thing as *too* paranoid.

"Not hungry, baby?" Koko asked. "Can I try one? Those look scrumptious."

I shook my head and smiled.

"No, I was just appreciating the plating," I said, spooning up a dumpling. "Everything Disco does is such art."

I snuck a glance in Disco's direction. He was completely absorbed in a conversation with someone to his left. Really, if he wanted to poison me, it'd be in my serving of Tiny Dancer, I reasoned.

So when I tasted an unusually sweet tang in the filling when I took my first silky bite, I attributed the flavor to Disco's chef getting weird again. The man once made fizzy rocks carbonara. Ever felt candied pancetta crackle and pop between your teeth? I don't recommend it.

I was three dumplings in before whatever was in them took hold. My first clue that something was amiss was the bugs made of pure electricity marching on a million sparking feet up and down my arms.

Then colors began to run together like ice cream and the chandelier belted out showtunes in an impressive baritone, drowning out all other noise. Koko squinted at me with his five glittering eyes and it was then that I realized I was talking. I was talking way too quickly and loudly about mermaids and robots and the ruined, oily sand along the Los Angeles coast.

"Poor dear," Disco hummed. "She's had such a rough time. I shouldn't have pushed her to come out again after how hard she's been working herself. I'd better get her to a bed."

My vision narrowed to a pinprick and I felt the icy hands of whatever he had drugged me with fold around my consciousness.

❋

When I came to, I thought I was staring at mossy rocks. Then my blurred vision corrected itself, and Disco's wide eyes took form inches from my face. A breathing mask covered the lower half of his face, which I thought was a strange thing to wear at a dinner party until I realized three things: One, I also had a mask on; two, we were out in the open ocean, alone; and three, we were definitely not at a clambake. A hurricane battered the sea above us. I turned my head as much as I was able to look up and around. We were so remote that I could barely make out the far-off lights of Electric Blue Moon winking through the haze.

I tried to swim forward to push Disco out of my way and discovered a fourth fact: The lying scrot had bound me by the wrists to a rocky outcropping. Fifth thing: Disco had dressed me in a goddamned sequined purple mermaid getup.

"What's the idea here, Disco? Or should I call you Winter?" At least he'd activated the localized coms in the masks.

"So, you uncovered my past. A little of it, at any rate. Good for you. What's the idea? You tell me, honey." Disco narrowed his eyes. "You can't really be satisfied playing the role of glorified sanitation worker for these people, day in and day out? Knowing that your life here continues only so long as you serve the right people? The trash you dig up might be more fun than what gets flushed down the toilet, but it stinks just the same."

"I'll take living an honest life over putting a bullet in someone's brain any day."

"Honest? You? Oh, spare me your sanctimony! And at any rate, Rocket—the Rocket you grew up with—was already dead. You figured out that much at least, right? You had to."

"So you're saying it's all right because you were murdering *androids* and not humans?"

"I had no part in his demise, but Rocket was long gone by the time I deactivated his synth. You can't murder a machine, seabunny."

"Lexi Lagoon might beg to differ on that point."

Disco rolled his eyes. "Even if you shot me dead right now, I'd be walking amongst the living again in two weeks flat with nearly every memory intact. I'd be at one hundred percent if you forgot to crush my body's black box. Inconvenient? Sure. But in no way is deactivation permanent."

"And Campari?"

"All right, you got me there." Disco sighed heavily, as though filled with regret. Somehow, I couldn't muster any sympathy for the guy. "She was threatening to spill a lot of dangerous, half-baked theories that would put too many eyes on my work here. I didn't expect *you* to be in attendance, of all people. And then you went and got yourself arrested at the scene of the crime! I'm forever grateful for the diversion you created. No one noticed *me* there at all. But I suppose if I think about it, that was really so Marrow of you. You do like your sticky situations, don't you?"

"So why'd you do it, Disco? Competition in the hab energy business? Sealliance send you out to do their dirty work and off the Nightingales' son to send a message?"

Disco laughed in my face, cold and mean.

"Your mommy's in way over her head in *that* world, baby. But yes, Sealliance does have a message for her."

"Sealliance is taking out competitors before they can make any real moves," I said. Disco did a slow clap and chuckled.

"Electric Blue Moon's ace detective cracks it! But like I said, that's not the only reason why I'm here."

"So why, then?"

"My, my, Marrow. You're so slow on the pickup tonight."

"Well, someone did drug my food."

He flashed a smile. "If only you'd just taken the Tiny Dancer. You could be higher than the moon right now and none the wiser. Think, Marrow! Do you honestly believe that the powers that be let a total nobody science-bot like Lexi just quit their job, swan off to a rival hab and take over a strip club? Sealliance put an astronomical bounty out on Lexi and Charisma. Rocket's intervention and political influence bought them time, but not much of it. And he only stepped in because he realized what those two were actually capable of."

"Synthetic mermaid bodies for anyone who can afford it," I said, remembering the schematics on Lexi's computer.

"Got it in one. Perfecting the transference of human consciousness into synthetic minds and bodies. That was always Rocket's endgame, his pet project. He wanted to do away with physical human bodies altogether. Can you imagine? No more need for habitats! The oceans would swell with thousands of the insufferable and the wealthy in their pursuit of a new Atlantis. It would be the Ceres debacle all over again."

"They're trying to create an entirely new species," I realized.

Disco nodded. "Lexi and Charisma were helping him because it was that or straight back to corporate slavery."

"And that's why? That's why you finished off Krill Intentions and made straight for our hab? Seduced Rocket? Just to get under his skin before you destroyed him?"

"Oh no, not at all. I did all that because I wanted a taste of an independent life. The longer I keep doing these dirty jobs for Sealliance, the less time I have to spend back in a lab. I mean in that way, we're strangely alike, don't you think?"

"Last time I checked, I don't remember murdering anyone to get an extra hall pass."

Disco scoffed.

"Don't try to be funny. You were born topside, yes? Do you even remember what it was like? The way folks cling to myth? They all believe that if they just go to the right coastal city, pray to the right gods, make the right sacrifices, they'll have a shot at something better below the waves. That they'll never again have to watch their friends and family immolated in a wall of fire or watch one of the last herds of cute, fluffy cows melt to death in a toxic rainstorm."

I did remember. My mother and father prayed nightly to Stella Maris—Our Lady, the Star of the Sea. They placed a wrinkled gold-foil picture of Her on a cinderblock altar, surrounded by little LED votives that flickered in salvaged seashells painted with crosses and neon stars.

"Do you know what happens to those like me, and Lexi, and Charisma once more fuckers like the Xashas and the Nightingales of the world get what they want? We end up lying in the broken shells of our bodies at the bottom of the ocean floor, waiting for a salvage crew to come pick us up and put us back together again. They don't turn off our pain sensors, Marrow.

"I was giving you a chance. You've always been one of the good ones, looking out for others, treating even the most menial workers with respect. When I took out Rocket, I called you first hoping you'd realize what he was doing and kick this wide open, hunt it down to the end like you always do. Then they covered up the whole thing—"

"You thought I'd *appreciate* that?" I was so stunned I stopped working the ropes for a moment.

"You're supposed to be this great private investigator! I wanted to give you something worthy to investigate!"

"Brother, I make a living taking dirty photos of people who failed to read their prenup. Sherlock Watson I ain't."

The storm picked up, whipping tendrils of our hair into a frenzy as flotsam and jetsam swirled past.

"Well that's a shame, truly. I'm disappointed in you, Marrow. But no matter."

I didn't like the finality in his voice. I pulled harder on the ropes. "What do you mean 'no matter?'"

"I mean I've got a job to do and intend to see it done. Farewell, Marrow Nightingale. I enjoyed knowing you for a little while."

"You're just gonna leave me out here to die? Bound to a rock?"

"I'm saving your life!"

That galled. "Really? From here it seems that you've drugged me, kidnapped me, tied me up in this ridiculous getup in the middle of a goddamned Pacific storm."

"Sure, but at least you're not at my clambake."

My blood went cold. *Koko.* "And why is that a good thing?" I managed to ask.

"There's been reports of a wild pack of wolf sharks in the area, hadn't you heard?"

We all knew the stories divers brought back of sleek, eerily intelligent sharks that hunted in cooperative packs. I was dubious they actually existed, but if you'd asked me a week prior about secret androids walking among us, I'd have said the same thing.

"Those are just old hab legends," I argued, but the malicious glint in Disco's eyes said that wasn't quite right.

"You'd be amazed at what brilliant minds have wrought down here among the habs! One little mistake can really fuck up an ecosystem. The pack will provide just the distraction I need to keep HabSec busy while I power down the hab hull and blow up all of your life support systems."

"Disco! Damnit, you don't have to do this!" I struggled against the ropes, not caring now if he figured out what I was trying to do.

"You'll thank me later," he said, just before he pulled out the shark prod and stunned me unconscious.

"Is that her?"

"Think so.

"Marrow! Hey, Marrow! Are you alive? Please say you're alive."

Lexi and Charisma swam up from behind me and looked me over. Lexi's face was the picture of worry; Charisma's skin pulsed a cacophony of distress. Lexi had dressed for the occasion in all black, their long hair pulled into an efficient, thick rope of a braid down the length of their back. Somehow, even their tail had shifted to a darker shade of rainbows and the shine on those scales seemed to promise death to any who touched it.

I squinted and wiggled experimentally against the rock. Aside from a throat raw from screaming, I seemed more or less alright. "Yeah, mostly. Drugged, though—not by choice."

Lexi snorted and said dryly, "Surprised any drugs get through that pickled liver of yours."

Charisma got the ropes off me in a hot second and I stretched my limbs, giving my wrists a shake.

"It's Disco, but there's no time to explain," I said, already swimming towards the hab in pursuit "We haven't got long. He's going after the power box for the hab's hull and the life support systems."

"You read our note!"

"That was you two? I thought you booked it when you saw me at Campari's that night."

"Well, you *are* the kind of lady who likes to make a bit of a scene, Marrow," Charisma said. "Our operation calls for a little more subtlety."

"We were there to broker a deal with Campari."

"What kind of deal?" We were swimming at my top speed which, given the storm and the drugs in my system, was not very fast. The hab seemed maddeningly far away still. I grunted and pushed my muscles harder.

Lexi filled me in as we swam. "She wanted to be next in line for a permanent merbody. Rocket had made the mistake of swimming out to the yacht wreck a few days ago. We had fitted him with a new lower torso to test, and that nosy sea hag happened to be there with all her camera gear, doing some sort of fashion editorial shoot."

"Not only that, but she had already figured out that Disco was Winter Mason, the sole survivor of the explosion at Krill Intentions," Charisma added. "She wanted to do a big reveal story on Disco, but of course Disco was not about to let that happen."

"That's what he and Rocket were fighting over," I mused.

"Rocket didn't know Disco was Sealliance's top assassin until he told us about the fight. He genuinely loved his fiancé. But when he found out the truth, he realized his entire relationship had been a lie so that Disco could get close to the Nightingales . . ."

"So Disco killed him in their own home."

"He had died—*really* died—some weeks before that incident," Lexi said softly.

The pain in my throat was unbearable, and it wasn't from all the screaming. "How?" I managed to ask.

"Does it matter?"

"Yes, it fucking matters!" I paid for that outburst as my lungs seized up and I coughed hard into my oxygen mask.

"He died helping us," Charisma said finally. "When we arrived at Electric Blue Moon, Lexi was injured and I was shot to hell. Sealliance's contractors were right on our tails, literally. Rocket answered our distress call and went out beyond the hab walls to fight them off himself. We made it inside, but he took one too many bullets in the process."

"I see." Of course he'd died heroically defending them.

"We brought him back once. It's fully possible we'll still be able to bring him back again, eventually," Lexi said softly. "Disco destroyed his black box, but there are memory backups we can use. We just need more time . . ."

"We're here," I said abruptly. I pushed away the feeble hope of getting my brother back and pried a loose panel up to expose a sea-filled tunnel that led into the hab's murky heart—the life support system, cooled by a continual current of chilly Pacific sea water. Disco hadn't bothered to cover his tracks very well. "We don't have much time; he's got a distraction planned on the other side of the hab to call HabSec out there. Once he has a clear path to the core, he's going to take it."

"Then we'd better hurry after him, hadn't we?" Lexi said.

They dove in first and Charisma followed close behind, wrapping a tentacle around my arm to pull me in after. Halfway down the tunnel, the lights went out. Disco must have made it.

We strained to swim as hard as we could through a maze of orange emergency lights and warning sirens. The tunnel spit us out into a cavernous room in the heart of Electric Blue Moon's core. The core was bigger than I had imagined, cavernous with a brutal echo to its many moving parts. The power sources cooled inside large pools of pumped-in sea water. At the far end of the room on a platform above one of the pools, we saw Disco fiddling with a control panel.

"There you three are," he said. His voice echoed through the room. "Very thoughtful of you, really. When Sealliance collectors retrieve my body, they'll be able to scrape yours up off what's left of the floor, too, and I'll get the bounty when they resurrect me."

"And what does a robot slave need with a bounty from

their manufacturer, exactly?" I asked. "You saving up for early retirement or something, Disco?"

"You can just go ahead and die right now, Marrow. You've gone from fun to annoying in record time."

He pointed a gun at us and unceremoniously took a shot. I dodged back under the water and when I came up a few feet away, Lexi and Charisma had already vanished.

"So, this is your job?" I called, ducking another bullet. I sloshed to the shallow end of the pool and hid behind a large, steel pipe. "Murdering the competition so your creators can continue to rule the seas and space unchallenged?"

"They're doing good work, Marrow. Work so important you couldn't possibly comprehend it from the bottom of that bottle you're always swimming in. When people like the Nightingales get ideas into their heads of working *against* Sealliance instead of *with* us as fairly paid contractors, that's just wasting time. That's wasting *the future.* And in a way, that's like murdering the future. It's like murdering billions of unborn futures. Doesn't that sound wrong to you?"

"Disco, the only thing sounding funny to my ears right now is you. Did you hit your head breaking into this place or did Sealliance just program this crazy into your core personality?"

I peeked out for a glance, and he responded with another bullet. That one pinged off of a pipe less than a foot away from my head—far too close for my liking. I looked around Lexi or Charisma or something I could use against Disco to neutralize him.

"It's a shame you see it like that, baby," Disco said. "You always seemed a little smarter than the others. Better head on your shoulders."

"And look where that got me: dodging bullets from a haute couture murder doll."

I was sweltering inside my wetsuit. Disco had deactivated the turbines that circulated the sea water around the engines, and the standing water was pulling in all the excess heat. If we didn't do something fast, we'd boil to death long before the hab blew. A pressure sensor alarm blared to life, and I used the noise to cover the sound as I leapt from my hiding spot to the rails of a nearby walkway. I climbed over and slid onto the metal flooring, catching my breath.

A panel repair box lay by my side. I pushed the lid off and dug through, trying to ignore the intermittent sound of bullets as Disco attempted to suss out where the three of us had got to. My hand closed around a large wrench and I took it with me as I crawled along the walkway, trying my best to stay low and quiet.

"Charisma, I don't know if they'll be able to repair you, unfortunately," Disco was saying. "Lexi is easy enough to fit with a new body, but you? You're organic. One of a kind. Or you were, until Sealliance decided to green light your prototype. Now there's like twenty octopuses like you working at the central hab. You could get turned into calamari by an angry mob for all Sealliance cares now. Though of course, they would very much prefer you returned to them alive."

"You and Sealliance can both pucker up and suck my mantle cavity!" Charisma called from somewhere above us.

Disco responded by firing up into the dark rafters and pipes. I heard Charisma chuckle and took that as my cue. I hauled the large wrench up and swung it over the railing. I was aiming for Disco, but it hit the control panel in front of him instead, which erupted in a shower of sparks and warning beeps.

Charisma took the opportunity to drop from the ceiling onto Disco's head at the same time that Lexi burst out of the water close by. They gripped the railing and swung their tail up over the side, slicing their shimmering dorsal fin in an arc that left a bloody red gash across Disco's throat. Disco spluttered and choked, then fell to the ground. I rushed over to join them.

"What the fuck?" I gasped for breath. "You two did not make up that move just now."

"How do you think we escaped Sealliance in the first place, Detective?" Charisma asked. She pressed several buttons on a nearby control console in quick succession and soon the alarms quieted down.

Lexi pulled out a small knife and expertly cut out the black box from the back of Disco's neck.

"Come on, we've got to get out of here," Lexi said. "HabSec is on the way with engineers. They can handle the repairs from here, but we can't be around when they find Disco. Too many questions."

I nodded, giving Disco one last parting look. How long would he stay dead this time, I wondered? We slipped back through the maintenance tunnel right as the main lights in the engine room came back online.

Back at the Kraken Club, we sat on the rooftop deck normally reserved for parties and Charisma poured me a stiff drink. I snuggled deeper into one of the plush robes they had on hand for their two-legged dancers to wear between performances.

"Congrats on saving the day, detective," she said.

The victory felt hollow. I couldn't even make a quip about Disco stiffing me on my fee. I was glad to be alive, but Rocket was still dead—*had* been dead without my realizing it—and even if they could bring him back, I didn't want to be a part of *that* world.

"There's a place for you in our vision of things, if you want it," Lexi said, as if reading my mind. I was quiet for a time, tugging at the frayed thoughts brushing the edges of my mind.

Eventually I asked, "You ever hear the old story about Zeus and Athena?"

Lexi just looked at me, waiting for me to continue.

"Old god Zeus, king of all the gods, gets this vision of his perfect woman. He's surrounded by women which a lot of us might call perfect: Hera, Aphrodite, Artemis. Each and every one of them glorious and worshipped. But Zeus? He's thinking: *All these great women around me, but they've got this one annoying trait I just can't work around; this one thing even I, Zeus the Almighty, can't control.*"

I took a pull from my vape and let the smoke out slow. I stared up at the beams and domes of Electric Blue Moon, at all the little ways the founding architects had tried their damnedest to build their old world into this new one. They'd tried to eliminate the parts they didn't like, but they ended up with a heap of shoddy replicas from the bygone days of an abandoned world.

"Free will," I said. "Independent thought. Zeus is supposed to be king of the gods, but his wife Hera won't even let him fuck peasant girls. Artemis is out there turning hunters into bears for sport. Aphrodite, well, we all know her story in some way or another. Zeus is just like: Fuck! These women. These uncontrollable women who would be perfect if they just . . . thought exactly like me and did what I said. So Zeus draws up a schematic and pulls from his big god brain . . ."

"Athena." Charisma finishes.

"Bingo. Athena. Sprung fully formed from Zeus's head. World's first android, if you ask me."

Charisma blinked thoughtfully, but Lexi's tone was ice. "We *escaped* Sealliance of our own volition."

"Did you? Athena did a lot of stuff Zeus didn't command her to do, but at the end of the day, when it came to war? She always was his right-hand general. And it seems to me Sealliance let you go awfully easy."

Lexi was quiet for a moment, then looked back at me. "I don't recall humans ever coming out on top in those stories about Zeus, either. Do you?"

"No, I sure don't." I pocketed my smoke and stood up. "Hell, forget I said anything. You did it; you got free from Zeus. Congrats, kids. But there's no place for me here anymore, either way. Some kind of war's coming, and I'm not keen on being in the middle when that hurricane hits."

"It's a big ocean, detective, but not that big. Where are you going to go?"

I looked up at the hab dome again. I thought of my birth parents, eagerly signing up to work for the Nightingales in hopes of a better life for me. Is this what they would have wanted for me, truly? How were they to know? How was anyone topside to know that the only thing waiting for them beneath the sea was a lifetime of servitude and an omnipresent threat of being spat out into the flames for the slightest misstep? Seemed like a big fucking scam, if you asked me.

And I was done waiting for that deportation notice to finally hit my inbox.

"Everyone keeps telling me I should take some time off. I'm thinking it's time I took that advice."

Carmen and Kline Nightingales' bodies were found floating a few miles from Fashima's Escape. Well, it certainly explained why they hadn't been returning my calls. An engine malfunction in their pleasure cruiser was the official report, and for once, I was content to let the coroner have the last word.

Especially not after I was informed of the contents of their wills, updated a mere twenty-four hours before their unfortunate accident. Coincidence? Maybe. They were getting on in years and their eldest son had just (allegedly) died. It made sense they would want to reallocate his inheritance. What didn't make sense was how they reportioned it.

> *The majority of the Nightingale holdings, businesses, investments, and properties are to be transferred to a private trust under the guidance of Palaimon Life Systems, in the interests of furthering advancements in robotics and aquatic engineering. To their daughter and sole heir, Marrow Nightingale, they bequeath a cash sum of five million doubloons.*

A payout for me to go quietly on my merry way, and all other funds devoted to their new big project, in other words. I wondered if Mom and Dad were already out there somewhere, swimming around in their new synthetic mer-bodies, or if they'd opted for something a bit more discrete. Well, five million was certainly enough to keep me tucked away somewhere comfortable for a lifetime. The thing was, comfortable things never sat quite right on my shoulders. I just didn't have the build.

Fashima's Escape Habitat
December 5, 2112

A chorus of bleeps and dings from slot machines played constant backdrop to the lo-fi death metal that piped through the casino café's speakers. A waiter in a clear plastic minidress and houndstooth thong combo set a cappuccino in front of me. I smiled up at him over the top of my datapad, which was currently scrolling a trashy romance novel about a Martian who falls in love with a Surfacer wasteland warlord.

"Is that the new *Bad Boy Oil Barons of Mars* I see?" a soft, cultured voice behind me asked.

I smirked and shut off the datapad, stashing it in my bag. "Just released last week."

My contact came around the side of the table and sat across from me. I knew her only as *Jane 05* and an encrypted signal and response that her com sent to mine. She set down a manila folder and slid my cappuccino across the table towards her. She helped herself to a dainty sip and smiled.

"I look forward to reading it myself, when I can find the time. This drink, unfortunately, is awful."

"Feel free to give it back." She smiled coyly over another sip and I nodded to the folder. "Were you able to find everything I asked for?"

"All that you asked for . . . and a little bonus besides."

I opened the folder to a grainy greenscale photograph.

My mother, in profile and wearing sunglasses but unmistakably her, alive and well. The timestamp on the photo placed it three days ago. I closed the folder.

"Where was this taken?"

"Right here in Fashima's Escape, love. She's a shy one, though. Took me a week's surveillance to get that shot. The details are in the file."

"Excellent work."

She laughed. "Not to be blunt, but you're paying double my going rate. I make a point to stand out to someone who can easily cover my living expenses for the next year with a single surveil and snap job."

I took the hint and sent the remainder of her fee over to her com. She glanced at it long enough to accept, then finished my cappuccino and stood up. "I'll be in town a bit longer, should you need anything else. Pleasure doing business with you."

The waiter rematerialized at my elbow as soon as I was alone.

"Your suite is ready for you now, Ms. Nightingale. Can I get you anything else?"

I picked up the folder and tucked it into my bag. "Yeah. Send up a bottle of your best seaweed gin. And flag my room as *Do Not Disturb* indefinitely."

I didn't plan to leave until I knew what my not-so-dead parents were up to, and I had a feeling this was going to take a while.

About the Author

Mia V. Moss is a speculative fiction author from the Pacific Northwest, now living in the SF Bay area. Her short stories have been published in *Cat Ladies of the Apocalypse, StarShipSofa, Galactic Stew*, and elsewhere. When she's not writing, she enjoys running around feral outdoors, DMing tabletop campaigns, mixing cocktails for friends, and admiring her enormous TBR pile. *Mai Tais For the Lost* is her debut novella.

She can be reached at www.magicrobotcarnival.com or on Twitter & Instagram @atomicjackalope.

Printed in Great Britain
by Amazon